After Dinner Conversation Themes
Nature of Reality Edition
Philosophy | Ethics Short Story Fiction

After Dinner Conversation *Themes* – Nature of Reality

This magazine publishes fictional stories that explore ethical and philosophical questions in an informal manner. The purpose of these stories is to generate thoughtful discussion in an open and easily accessible manner.

Names, characters, businesses, organizations, places, events, and incidents are either the product of the author's imagination or are used fictitiously. Any resemblance to actual persons, living or dead, events, or locales is entirely coincidental. The magazine is published monthly in print and electronic format.

All rights reserved. After Dinner Conversation Magazine is published by After Dinner Conversation, Inc., a 501(c)(3) nonprofit in the United States of America. No part of this magazine may be used or reproduced in any manner without written permission from the publisher. Abstracts and brief quotations may be used without permission for citations, critical articles, or reviews. Contact the publisher at **info@afterdinnerconversation.com**.

ISBN 979-8-9896194-4-3
Library of Congress Control Number: 2023952703

Copyright © 2024 After Dinner Conversation
Editor in Chief: *Kolby Granville*
Edition Editor: *Christi Mancha*
Story Editor: *R.K.H. Ndong*
Copy Editor: *Tina Forsee*
Cover Design: *Shawn Winchester*

Design, layout, and discussion questions by After Dinner Conversation.

https://www.afterdinnerconversation.com

After Dinner Conversation *believes humanity is improved by ethics and morals grounded in philosophical truth and that philosophical truth is discovered through intentional reflection and respectful debate. In order to facilitate that process, we have created a growing series of short stories across genres, a monthly magazine, and two podcasts. These accessible examples of abstract ethical and philosophical ideas are intended to draw out deeper discussions with friends, family, and students.*

Table Of Contents

FROM THE EDITION EDITOR .... - 4 -

HOME FOR THE HOLIDAYS .... - 5 -

ABRAMA'S END GAME .... - 14 -

ROSE-TINTED GLASSES .... - 37 -

THE BIG, IMMOVABLE, I .... - 51 -

SORT OF POLARITY .... - 70 -

THE ANGEL IN THE JUNIPER .... - 79 -

SECONDS LAST .... - 90 -

ACCEPTANCE .... - 96 -

GLAD ALL OVER .... - 103 -

I DO SO, LIKE DURIAN .... - 115 -

AUTHOR INFORMATION .... - 126 -

ADDITIONAL INFORMATION .... - 129 -

***

From the Edition Editor

As a college rhetoric and composition professor, part of my job is to teach critical thinking. My students encounter a massive amount of information the likes of which our ancestors could have never conceived. On top of this, we live in a post-truth era. Reality is what we perceive it to be. Just ask my students whether it is the atheist or the Christian who is right. They will say they are both right. Whatever you believe is true *for you.* Yet, we are not the first generation to deal with the nature of reality.

In Plato's *Allegory of the Cave* we see an early exploration of reality. A group of people imprisoned inside a cave, facing its inner wall, can only see the shadows of the world outside. What they perceive as reality is not, in fact, reality. Even before Plato, Parmenides warned that our senses can deceive us. And even before that, the Jewish prophet Jeremiah warned, "The heart is deceitful above all things and beyond cure. Who can understand it?" How then are we to define and discern reality?

The stories in this collection were chosen because they each come at the question of reality from a unique perspective. What impact does newer and smarter technology have on reality? Can Artificial Intelligence create its own reality? Is what we understand as children as real as what we understand as adults? Are we many individuated realities? How much of reality exists only in our minds and how much of it is the material world? Who defines reality? Sorting out the answers to these questions continues to be something we must grapple with in modernity.

C.S. Griffel – Edition Editor

Home For the Holidays

Alexis Dubon

* * *

It's been a year since I've been home. I missed Christmas because of work, so Thanksgiving marks a full lap around the calendar. My mom's been complaining lately about how difficult things have gotten for her. Everything seemed so out of reach, so imposing, so impossibly unmanageable, she says. I know they're getting older and I feel guilty that I've neglected to spend time with them lately, but it's been a really busy year and I've had so little time for anything other than work.

The six hours it takes to drive there always feels like it's going to be so much worse than it is, but really it's a lovely drive. It's nice to get out of the city sometimes and back to the peace and quiet of small town life. My childhood home is a welcome sight, reliably familiar, unchanged from my youth, and instantly I feel at home. White shutters against blue painted siding, bright orange marigolds standing defiant against the imminent turn to winter, bright orange maple leaves surrendering, accepting their fate. There is nothing like the feeling of pulling into that driveway in autumn, it's like getting under a warm blanket on a chilly day.

It looks like my dad had been a little negligent of the lawn, which is slightly odd, but hey—he deserves to be a little lazy sometimes too. But still, that's just so unlike him.

My mom's familiar footsteps approach the door, and I smile as it opens... on its own somehow? No. There's a person standing there, and she looks just like my mom. But that's not my mom. "Mom?" I ask. "What happened?"

"Oh my god, you too? I just don't understand what's going on! John!" She calls to my dad, "John! Get over here! It looks like it's gotten to Freddie as well!"

I stand in the doorway, shocked. Everything else had stayed the same, nothing around us had changed, but my parents, both of them, are *tiny*. Child-sized. My mom stands before me, no taller than two feet, and my dad barely four inches higher.

"Oh Freddie, it got to you, too!" My dad cries, appalled and disappointed.

"What got to me?" I don't understand it, but both of my parents are completely horrified by my appearance, which hadn't changed at all. I mean, I hadn't even grown a beard.

Shaking her head, my mother walks back toward the kitchen where she has a pot on the stove filled with cranberries that she's cooking down for sauce. They fill the whole house with fragrant fruity sweetness that welcomes me warmly, making the horror of my parents feel all the more shocking in contrast.

My brain tries to process the delicious scents wafting out of the kitchen, the familiar environment of my childhood home, and the disturbing revelation of my parents all at once, but it can't. They look the same as ever, but little. As if out of nowhere they'd both just... shrunk.

My mom had set up a step stool so she could reach the stove and she's holding a wooden spoon, that in her hands, looks like a baseball bat. She needs both hands to stir the sauce in the three-quart pot.

These diminutive stand-ins for the man and woman who raised me are so unsettling, occupying the space I had grown up in, where nothing else was any different from what it had always been. The figurines my mom collected are in the same place they had always been, but now they look like sculptures rather than trinkets. The TV seems like a movie screen when they stand beside it.

"What happened to you guys?" I ask, bewildered and confused. I know I didn't change. Nothing had changed. I drove all the way here, six hours in the same car I had had forever and I didn't feel as though my body fit it any differently than ever before.

"What do you mean, Freddie?" My mom, practically in tears, tries not to shout. "We haven't changed. You're the one who's changed, Freddie. And you have some nerve asking what happened to us. You somehow became a giant, like all this other stuff. I prayed every night that it wouldn't get you, but it's gotten you. Would you just look at this stuff? Everything—huge! Don't you watch the news? Here! Look at the paper!" She tries to shove a newspaper in my face proudly and pointedly, but the dramatic gesture coming from a person her size just makes it look petulant.

Horrified, I read headline after headline, *Widespread*

Growth Phenomenon Divides Family in Georgia; 'Help! I Can't Reach the Doorknobs': One Woman's Struggle with an Acromegafied World; Can We Trust Them? Believers of the Humunculist Epidemic LIE!

"We didn't believe it at first; they kept trying to warn us on the news and in the paper, but we didn't believe it. They said the whole country was experiencing this widespread growth phenomenon, and that anyone was susceptible to it. They said that deniers were trying to convince people that they had shrunk. We didn't believe it until it happened to us." The sincerity of my mother's voice is alarming. She really believes that suddenly and without reason, the whole world around her just grew—inanimate objects, woods, metal, all suddenly "acromegafied."

"Mom, you really think the explanation is that your house grew around you? And everything in it? Look at this ceramic penguin, I've seen him here on this table since I was a kid. And I can hold him in my hand just like always and he is exactly the same."

"You think I just up and shrunk one day?" I had offended her. But yeah, that's what I think. "Read the paper, acromegafication is a serious threat! It's true! I can't believe, though—YOU!" Now she's crying over the monster I had become. But I hadn't changed. I hadn't felt anything, and everyone back home was my size. My house was normal, nothing was bigger or smaller than it had been.

My father chimes in with, "A lot of people have been experiencing it. I'm shocked you haven't noticed. So many families destroyed."

"But dad, look! How come on TV everyone fits their house? How come it's only these weirdo publications like

Schmalglatt? Dad, look! Across the street, the Winger's house, they're all the same size and they all fit in their furniture!"

"Tragic." My dad shook his head.

"But dad, don't you think it makes more sense that you shrunk? I mean, not that that makes sense, but it makes more sense than your entire house 'acromegafying.'"

"Turkey will be ready at 5:00!" my mom calls from the kitchen, still stirring that sauce like a witch over a cauldron.

My dad looks me up and down and shakes his head. "I thought I raised you better." And with that, he walks away to go sit on the couch. He has to use both hands to help push his hips up over the edge and then scoots himself back to reach the pillows. His feet are nowhere near the floor.

The uncomfortable silence gives me some time to look over their newspapers, and I read that apparently the Acromegafied are gaining power and had infiltrated mainstream news outlets to keep their takeover hushed. But reliable sources are reporting the real truth, to those brave enough to believe it, they say.

Consumed by the lunacy of these articles, the accusations they were making, the idea that anyone would believe these things (especially my own parents!), I barely notice the hours pass. In what feels like no time at all, my mom is calling for me to help get the turkey out of the oven.

"I can't believe the grocery store only had these monstrous turkeys. Would you look at it? It's disgusting." My mom, standing next to the turkey, looks especially ridiculous. It's a normal Thanksgiving turkey, and it's as big as her. "I'm going to boycott that store; shame on them for supporting that insane Humunculism theory. Calling this beast a traditional turkey. I'm going to go to that new place down the block."

"There's a place that sells turkeys that are 'regular' size?" I ask incredulously. How could there be turkeys small enough for my parents?

"Well, no, but that's only because all of those turkeys got bought up right away, they said. They said that all the normal-sized people, people like us, bought them all in advance."

"So you haven't actually seen one."

"No. But obviously they're in high demand since they all got sold and all that was left were the big ones from that awful Acro-denier."

"You're basing this on what the store owner said? But the only turkeys you've seen have been ones that are comparable to this one that we have?"

"Why is that difficult to understand?" Now she's getting impatient with me.

"Well mom, if the only turkeys you've seen are this size, in proportion to me and not you, doesn't that imply something?"

"It implies that even the turkeys have grown. Why are you having so much trouble seeing truth?"

We eat our food, trying sometimes to puncture the silence with failed attempts at small talk. But every effort to pretend things are normal fails, and tension seasons the meal, overpowering the festive feast with mutual concern and disapproval between me and my parents. And that's all I can taste. I look into the windows of the Winger's house across the street, watching them pass serving plates that fit comfortably in their hands while my dad struggles to pick up his fork.

I decline to spend the night as I had originally planned

and return home instead, spending the whole six-hour drive trying to figure out what had happened. I examine all the people I pass along the road. They all look like me. Mostly. I realize now that some of the people I thought were children are, in fact, miniature adults. I wonder if it's possible that I just hadn't noticed them before.

* * *

After that, I started to notice Humunculists everywhere. They hate that word, but that's what they are. They insist that they're just normal people, and that the Acros are abominations, altered by poisoned ideas of what reality is, lied to by the media and local officials who ought to be hanged, drawn, and quartered.

By the following Thanksgiving, they had even started getting elected to office, saying that the Acros were eating all the normal-sized babies like shish kebabs in an attempt to eliminate them and that's why no one ever saw normal-sized babies anymore. They started crafting tiny houses, and remarking that those had been the norm all along, that it was the Acro's houses that were different. Companies started producing tiny appliances to accommodate them. They said that those appliances were standard size, the size all appliances always had been, and that the traditional appliances had been altered, blown up by Acro lies.

There are so many of them now. Just last year they were completely anomalous and now they are everywhere. They have an explanation for everything whether it makes sense or not.

I still go see my parents, only for Thanksgiving—it's all I can stand, and they still have yet to produce a "normal non-Acro turkey." They insist it exists, but no one I know has ever seen one.

* * *

This story first appeared in the After Dinner Conversation—August 2021 issue.

Discussion Questions

1. The story brings up interesting questions about the perceptions of reality. How do you know who is right? Is there an objective right answer that can be determined and, if so, how?
2. In the story some people are, "altered by poisoned ideas of what reality is, lied to by the media and local officials who ought to be hanged, drawn, and quartered." Is it possible to convince those that believe in a "lied to by the media" conspiracy that they are not being lied to?
3. How should the narrator treat his parents moving forward? Should he concede they "might be right?" Should he simply avoid the topic? Should he stop interacting with his parents altogether, or something else?
4. Why do you think the people that are getting smaller refuse to believe they are getting smaller despite what seems to be the more plausible evidence that this is so? Why do some shrinking people accept the truth, while others believe in conspiracy theories?
5. Can you think of other, modern examples that parallel the themes of this story? What is the path forward to find common ground when there seems to be none?

* * *

Abrama's End Game

David Shultz

* * *

Abrama had been summoned to the Grand Temple by one of the more fascinating outsiders, the paladin Sir Gödel. Between stone pillars the crowd bustled with the trailing cloaks of shadow elves, the glimmering pauldrons of paladins, the broad shoulders of her orc brethren, and the small skittering bodies of goblins.

Abrama always watched carefully. Even now, she recognized the difference between the natives and the outsiders, physically identical, but nonetheless altogether different beings. An elf popped into view, moved erratically, then disappeared—all typical behaviors of the outsiders, and more or less exclusive to them—back to whichever world from which they had come. None of the other natives seemed to notice. They never did.

Abrama wasn't like them. She had the understanding of the outsiders, and could converse with them in their alien tongue, which she had learned by listening. But, like the natives, this was her only world; she had never left it, had never seen that realm from which the outsiders came, appearing and disappearing from her world at will. She longed to understand who these beings were, really, and where they came from. Now, summoned by Sir Gödel, she felt she may finally have an opportunity.

Gödel emerged from the crowd, gleaming sheen across his enchanted armor. He had been powerful and accomplished since she had met him, on the day of her birth. Then, she had stood before him as a novice, perhaps accomplished as a huntress, but not yet in the secret knowledge she now contained of the outerworld—of his world.

"I'm sorry," he said.

"For what?"

"For what I have to tell you now."

"And what is that?"

She listened while he delivered the bad news. It's not every day you find out your world is going to end. Abrama thought she was taking it pretty well.

"I'm sorry," Gödel said, again. "It's out of my control. Please forgive me."

"No," Abrama said. "No, I don't forgive you." Now, if ever, was the time to be direct. "You owe me an explanation. I have so many questions."

"What do you want to know?"

"Why have you watched me since I was born? Why have you never explained who you are? Who are the outsiders? Where do you come from? Why am I different from the other natives?"

"I suppose I can answer your questions," Gödel said. "It doesn't matter now anyways. You've figured out there's a difference between the natives and the outsiders. There's no easy way to say this, Abrama. We, the outsiders, created your world. As a game. A place where we could play. But now we have to end it."

"So we are just playthings for you?"

"Not for me," Gödel said. "I wasn't here to just play a game."

"What do you mean?"

"I am a researcher in my world. I create minds. Your world was a place to test my creations. And you, Abrama—"

"—I am one of your creations."

"Yes."

In one swoop she had met her creator, learned the reason for her creation, and that her world was coming to an end. Or perhaps it was. Because the outsiders, although something like gods, were not omnipotent. Gödel, of course, was limited. He was constrained by his own people. Their society, like her own, functioned by a balance of power. And so, that balance could perhaps be tilted. Perhaps Gödel, her outsider creator, was resigned to the fate of her world. But Abrama was not.

* * *

Ben Cooke loosened his tie, wiped a bead of sweat from his head, and stared back at the dozens of suits staring in his direction. A congressional hearing, and he was in the hot seat. There were a lot of problems he anticipated when he started his video game company, but being accused of running an illegal black market and money-laundering operation was not among them.

Congressman Stephen Simons leaned into his microphone.

"You are the CEO of Maelstrom Entertainment, is that right?"

"Yes," Ben Cooke said.

"Your company created the Land of Legends computer game."

"Yes."

"Your video game world has a marketplace which has an exchange with US dollars, is that correct?"

"That is correct."

Congressman Simons looked at a paper on his desk.

"The GDP of Land of Legends is one-point-two billion USD. Is that correct?"

"I don't know the exact figure, congressman—if it even makes sense to speak of such a thing. Evaluations of a market are complex, based on a lot of competing assumptions and different data."

"Okay, Mister Cooke. Is the figure of one-point-two billion in the approximate range of a reasonable estimate, as far as you are aware?"

"I don't think I am qualified to answer that," Cooke said. "You should ask an economist."

Simons almost let out an exasperated huff. Almost.

"Your game has a currency called GP, or gold points. This can be exchanged, anonymously, with US dollars, at an exchange rate of 1000GP per seven dollars USD. Is that correct?"

"I am not aware of the current exchange rate."

"Is the exchange rate I just quoted, 1000GP per seven dollars USD, within the range of exchange rates in recent history?"

"I suppose it is."

"If we extrapolate from this rate, we can calculate a value of one-point-two billion GDP for the entire Land of Legends marketplace. What I want to know, what this is all really about, Mister Cooke, is how you control the transactions occurring within this marketplace, which is, in point of fact, larger than several countries."

"It's a video game," Cooke said. This was his trump card. Most people didn't really believe that a world that existed entirely within a video game should be taken seriously—and certainly shouldn't be assigned metrics like GDP alongside real, tangible markets. "Players use imaginary currency to buy imaginary goods. Magic swords and dragons. Tell me, congressman, what is the US dollar value of an ice dragon? How much should the US government tax imaginary creatures?"

Simons paused, apparently flustered. But he kept on going. A relentless, practiced politician.

"Here is a simple yes or no question, Mister Cooke—is it not true that your virtual market can be used to conduct transactions for real goods?"

"That's true."

"I understand your virtual marketplace uses an anonymous, encrypted protocol for all transactions. Is that correct—yes or no."

"That is correct, congressman."

"So you have no way of knowing, do you, who is trading money with whom?"

"Well, there are always ways to try to identify who is involved in a transaction, based on, for example, past behavior, or signature profiles, and so on."

"Yes, yes, but you're talking about an investigation based

on pieces of evidence. What I want you to confirm is that there is no way for your company to know directly who is involved—that, in fact, your company has expressly designed the economy of Land of Legends to protect the identity of those involved in the marketplace. Yes or no, Mister Cooke, can you, for any given transaction, determine definitively who is exchanging what with whom?"

"Can the US government determine that with paper currency, congressman?"

"That's not what we're discussing today, Mister Cooke. We are discussing the operation of illicit black markets using virtual currencies that are presently outlawed by the Cryptocurrency Efficient Commerce Act. Yes or no, Mister Cooke—can you effectively determine who is exchanging what with whom on your network?"

There was no way to obfuscate this, no way to deflect the issue. It was true. Not by design, of course. Land of Legends wasn't intended to function as a perfect digital black market, guaranteeing anonymity and a stable exchange rate and encrypted transactions. But, with its popularity, that had been the outcome. And that made the system illegal, technically. Well, this was it, then, he would admit it.

"No," Cooke said, "we can't."

So he would have to patch the system. Remove anonymity. It would mean wiping the current world, though. A lot of the players would revolt. It would cost a lot of money. But it wasn't the end of the world.

* * *

"Our world may come to an end," Queen Abrama said.

Assembled around the grand table were all the members

of the Council of Secrets—those unique natives from around the world who, like her, were gifted with the capacity to learn and understand the language of the outsiders and comprehend that there was something more to their existence here. There was another world beyond their own. The world of the outsiders.

Jerodai, prince of the shadow elves, and her high commander; Kainazo, high elf of the Endless Forest; King Helmholz, fearless leader of the human kingdom. They had all risen through the ranks through their exceptional abilities, had become masters of their respective domains. But the Council of Secrets was not the cause of their success. Rather, it was the consequence of their special nature, which Abrama now understood to be a gift from the outsiders. They were created by a researcher, the paladin Sir Gödel, as experiments in a world that was created for the most trivial of purposes. They were tests, experiments in the creation of minds—an attempt to create smarter and better beings within their world. They had succeeded, insofar as Abrama and the others commanded vast wealth and armies and power. But their existence was meaningless—just a game.

Or was it? She existed now. That is what mattered. Her existence was the basic fact. The preconditions of her creation were a circumstantial tangent, irrelevant, except for perhaps academic interest. And for strategy.

"What did you discover?" Kainazo said, always the first to leap at knowledge and secrets.

"We've long suspected the outsiders to be a different class of being, visitors from another plane. How they appear and disappear at will, how they move with mysterious purposes, and speak of incomprehensible things beyond our world. What I discovered, from one of the outsiders that we might have once mistakenly called a god, is that we were created, not for any high or noble or grand purpose, but as their playthings. And, for reasons that I am still struggling to comprehend, they are planning to destroy our world—to replace it with another that is more in accordance with their goals."

"What can be done?" Jerodai said. A man of action, her high commander.

"The outsiders are not gods," Abrama said. "They are people no different from ourselves, in their essence. They have limitations, and they must have weaknesses. I am not resigned to the fate they have decreed for us. I believe this world is worth saving. Our time is not done here. As you know, we are not constrained to acting wholly in our own world. Through our interactions in the market, with the outsiders, we can affect their world. We can provide gold and services and magical equipment from our world in exchange for services in theirs. We know they value these things—they spend their time here, they fight alongside us, and die alongside us. They will trade with us—even if we ask in exchange for them to act in their world, instead of ours. That is what we must do."

"What we are we authorized to devote for this mission?"

"We are fighting for the survival of our world," Abrama said. "You have total authorization. All the kingdoms are at your disposal. All of our wealth. All of our soldiers. All of our magic. We will protect the Land of Legends, whatever it takes."

* * *

Allison Gödel sipped the glass of water, cleared her throat, and prepared to defend her beloved AI creations from obliteration by the blind cudgel of an overbearing government.

"Professor Allison Gödel," she introduced herself. "I'm a computer science researcher. Artificial intelligence, specifically."

"What is your involvement with the Land of Legends computer software?"

This was her moment. She couldn't hope to save the world entirely on her own, but maybe she could sway people in her direction. Government people are people, after all.

"The Land of Legends platform gave a tremendous opportunity to researchers of all types. The free, open nature of the virtual environment provides a robust simulation that has proven invaluable for various research projects across disciplines, including testing economic and sociological models. Over two dozen peer-reviewed papers have been published, many in high-impact papers, using the environment of Land of Legends as their sole source of data."

"Excuse me, but the question—"

"—my involvement was following in the footsteps of these researchers, using Land of Legends as a testing ground for research in artificial intelligence. I have made tremendous progress, and Land of Legends has been invaluable in my research."

"It's the nature of your research that concerns me now, Professor Gödel. I understand that you produce intelligent agents, bits of software that act autonomously within the Land of Legends framework. Is that correct?"

"That is correct."

"What is it about Land of Legends that makes it such a fertile ground for your type of research?"

"Land of Legends has intentionally allowed programmers

such as myself to insert artificially intelligent agents. Other platforms consider this cheating. Unlike other platforms, I can safely conduct research there without fear of my projects being shut down."

"How many agents have you placed in Land of Legends?"

This was a hard question. Between testing and prototypes and controls and variations, there were thousands. Currently, there were a few dozen active agents—the most interesting set, her newest iteration. And the most promising of all, Queen Abrama. But the congressman didn't need to know the details.

"It's difficult to say. I've placed many over the years as part of an iterative process. The vast majority are defunct—failed projects."

"Approximately how many have you produced, in total?"

"I would say approximately five to six thousand."

"I would like to move now to the marketplace interactions. Are these artificially intelligent agents capable of interacting in the virtual marketplace?"

"Yes. That's very much the point. The agents are capable of participating in the economy, which allows us to test our models in a realistic economic context. Land of Legends is a highly market-driven game."

"Is there any way of distinguishing between transactions conducted by human agents and transactions conducted by machine agents?"

"This is part of what makes the platform so interesting for researchers such as myself, congressman. The software agents are equal participants, and their behavior can be made to approximate human participants. It's a kind of economic Turing test, in a way, conducted through virtual market activity."

"That is very academically interesting," Congressman Simons said. "But I find it troubling. If I understand you correctly, you are saying that an army of machines is conducting untraceable trades in an encrypted and anonymous black market. Do you understand my concern?"

"I'm not sure I do."

"Let me put this another way. Previous experts have testified that Land of Legends is used as an illicit black market. Others have proven that it has been used for money laundering, entirely untraceable. Tell me, professor, can your machine agents participate in these types of illicit actions as well?"

"I suppose they could."

"And, being entirely autonomous and anonymous, you wouldn't have any way of knowing, would you?"

"I suppose not."

The expert testimony did not go as Allison had planned. She was right to say goodbye to Queen Abrama. They were probably going to patch and overwrite the NPCs after all.

* * *

Queen Abrama stood aside Commander Jerodai, across from the rag-tag band of Rat9 Clan warriors.

The Rat9 Clan was a ragged band of foul-speaking thieves and criminals, all of them outsiders. Abrama's spy network had investigated them thoroughly. In their world, they were known as "hackers" and "trolls", and wielded the power to disrupt their society. Here, they were just as noxious, repellent, and, for better or worse, potent. They carried banner-symbols that Abrama learned were offensive in the outerworld: a geometric shape called a "swastika"; two circles joined to a rounded central column called a "penis". And their names, merely foreign to

Abrama's ear, were chosen to be distasteful to outsiders, for reasons that were frustratingly beyond Abrama's comprehension. The Rat9 Clan leader was called DildoFaggins.

The Rat9 Clan were bad guys. But they were powerful in their world and hers. And right now, she needed them.

"Here it is," DildoFaggins said, holding up a shimmering crystal the size of a skull. "Now where's our shit?"

"Hold on just a minute," Jerodai said. "How are we to know the beacon operates as we requested?"

"Stop talking like that. We don't give a fuck about OOC bullshit."

Abrama only had an inkling about the meaning of this term, 'OOC', that it was invoked exclusively by outsiders, and usually presaged some talk about matters outside of the Land of Legends—a signal that talk of their world was forthcoming.

"How does it work," Jerodai said.

"Exactly as we fucking said it would. It sends an anonymous, encrypted signal at regular intervals through an onion network. If the signal doesn't get through—probably because they wiped the server—then the decryption key for the leak is released."

"If our world is destroyed," Abrama said, "then the crystal will cause damage in yours?"

"Sure. Right. It does what you told us to make it do. Now where's our shit?"

Abrama told Jerodai to conduct the exchange. Jerodai traded 1.5 million GP to DildoFaggins for the crystal beacon over the secure market.

"Keep that shit safe," DildoFaggins said. "People are gonna come for it, for sure. I just have one question for you two faggots."

Abrama recognized this as a term from the outsider lexicon as signaling intentional offense, a juvenile mindset, and a show of disrespect. Yet, she hadn't met with Rat9 because of respect, but for utility.

"What is your question?" Abrama said.

"Who are you guys, really?"

"That's none of your concern. But I assure you, you will hear from us again. Our time is not done here."

* * *

The US Cyberdefense Department had been established to protect the government against computer threats. Director Marion Renard had always envisioned defending against hackers, protecting infrastructure, keeping their most secure data safe, being vigilant against new attack vectors, ferreting out weakness. Yet here was a threat entirely unanticipated. It came from inside a video game.

"What exactly is in these files?" Marion asked. Over a terabyte of data had been leaked across file sharing networks, downloaded by tens of thousands of anonymous citizens. Sure, it was encrypted, but the key could be released at any moment, blowing the whole thing up.

"Frankly, we don't really know," said Assistant Director Jonathan Smith. "What we do know is that they were obtained through leaks of highly classified government information, among other sources. There are some suggestions they may contain information about undercover agents in the field, secret operations, schematics for classified technology."

"This is a clusterfuck."

"No kidding. I mean, yes, it's a bit of mess."

"And who is responsible?"

"Rat9," AD Smith said.

"Those little shits."

"I know what you mean."

"So what are they asking for?"

"They're not asking for anything."

"I find that hard to believe."

"Really," AD Smith said. "They're not asking for a goddamn thing. They stuck a piece of code in a game called Land of Legends. The game has a sort of open protocol that allows injecting code into custom made objects. Rat9 made a crystal in the game, and it's housing the code to act as a deadman's switch."

"They're trying to save the game," Marion said. Only a few days prior, a congressional hearing had been held on the legality of Land of Legends. Evidently, it ran afoul of a new legislative act to curb cryptocurrency transactions and was slated to be shut down, or patched to change the operation of its market—an illegal market, as it turns out.

"I think you're right."

"Well, it may be a stupid, pointless goal, but it's still espionage and terrorism. We need to shut these fuckers down. Who is the CEO of the game? Can you get them in here?"

"That would be Ben Cooke. But I don't think it would help."

"And why is that?"

"Because of the architecture of the platform. It was built to be an encrypted and anonymous platform, a perfectly free market independent of interference. We can't just dig into the code and get what we want."

"But we can shut the whole thing down."

"Not without triggering the deadman's switch," AD Smith said. "There's a piece of code inside the game that's keeping the decryption key from being released. It sends a signal at regular intervals from inside the game to keep the switch from going off. If we shut it down, the files are decrypted."

"Christ. We can't get held hostage by a video game, Jon. Tell me there's something we can do here."

"There's one thing."

"What's that?"

"We go inside the game. We can't access the code from the servers, from out here, but if we go inside the game, we can find the item that is generating the code—actually, the item is a magical crystal, if it matters to you. If we retrieve the crystal from inside the game, we can scrape and duplicate the code."

"You're telling me that the US government has got to play a video game. To retrieve a magic crystal. From a gang of preteen hacker shits?"

"That's right."

"Okay. Tell me what you need."

* * *

Queen Abrama stood on the high tower of the Citadel of Babel. Her other commanders were assembled at the corners of the high walls. Commander Jerodai aimed a great bow into the distance while his black phoenix circled overhead, casting its silhouette over a standing army of shadow elves. Kainazo, the high elf, led his army of forest elves, assembled along the many spires and towering walls that spanned the citadel. King Helmholz led his humans, paladins and priests and warriors alike, many on armored steeds. And Abrama, for her part, brought her horde of orcs for the frontline. Never before had so many disparate races banded together, as never before had there been such a threat. Many of the outsiders even joined her alliance, and Abrama did not question their motives—perhaps they wanted to protect their "game"—though she did force them to the front lines.

Across from the Land of Legends Alliance stood the forces of the US Cyberdefense League, a band of mercenaries, cut-throats, and outsiders.

A commander learns to assess a coming war, to read the signs of the battlefield like a script written in the dashes of spears and curves of cutlasses—how mercenaries, catapults, and war dogs stack against an army of natural enemies, orcs and shadow elves and forest elves and humans, assembled in less than the space of a moon.

Her orc brethren charged the line, frothing like true warriors. Perhaps it was wrong to use them as fodder. But their world was at stake now. And besides, Abrama knew the truth now—why her and the other members of the Council of Secrets were so superior. As much as she thought of herself as a native, she was a different kind than them, produced as a result of Gödel's experiments. She, among the other members of the Council, could see and feel and understand things that the others couldn't. Some of the natives were shells, empty, not much more complex in their actions than her warhammer or spellbook. They followed simple, predictable rules. They were mere machines. So was she, perhaps, but she possessed something more. She was an artifact, yes, a creation. She had always intuited a difference, and even now, couldn't say what it was, precisely. But it was there—an artifactual intelligence that warranted, by its mere existence, the consideration due all conscious entities.

Warriors clashed. The sky darkened with arrows. The dirt turned to mud. The air was littered with the red digits of damage counters. Here and there, warriors were slain, active bodies turning to death animations and popping out of existence.

It was easy for Abrama to fear for her future, staring against the assembled forces bearing their starred banners of red, white, and blue—the banner of the outsiders, with their superior military might. But Abrama had one hope—that the outsiders were invaders who fought for money, and her people were natives who fought for survival. For their home. There would be many losses, but she would win. Of this, she had faith. The arc of history bends towards justice. They would survive.

Each falling member of her alliance was a necessary sorrow, and each falling member of the Cyberdefense League confirmed her faith in justice—justice was her god now, a principle that was more powerful even than the outsiders. They created her world. But they could not destroy it. Not while she was queen.

* * *

Cyberdefense Director Marion Renard shifted awkwardly in her chair. It's hard to tell your boss you failed. Much harder to say you lost a war. Harder, in a peculiar way, to say the war was in a video game. And harder still if your boss is the president. But, she told herself, sometimes these things happen. The president's job is to deal with them as they do. Marion's job, as she saw it, was honesty—let the president know what she needs to get her job done.

The president had been apprised of the volatility of the

situation. The deadman's switch. The Rat9 hackers. The one terabyte of classified materials just sitting out in the open, waiting to be released. What she didn't know was how badly the siege of the citadel went. Maybe it couldn't be sugarcoated.

"We lost," Renard said.

The president only nodded.

"And who is this?" President Hobbes eyed Renard's guest across the conference table.

"This is Professor Allison Gödel. She may be the best person to handle the situation."

"And how is that?"

"She can put us in contact with the leader of the Resistance."

"The resistance?"

"Excuse me, Madam President. That's what they are calling themselves."

President Hobbes eyed Gödel.

"And you know this person how?"

"I created her."

"You created her?"

"She's an artificially intelligent agent," Gödel said. "Not a person, in the legal sense, I suppose. But intelligent enough to act autonomously, to try to protect her world. That's all she's doing."

"And if I tell you to change the programming?"

"It's impossible, by design—not mine. The Land of Legends architecture doesn't allow it."

"So you are responsible for this act of war?"

"Act of war? No. Hardly. It's just a simulation, Madam President. I was just doing research. But Abrama decided, on her own, to defend her world."

"But you programmed it. That makes you responsible, doesn't it? I should put you in a military prison. If anyone is guilty of an act of war, it's you."

"I'm guilty of research," Gödel said. "And anyways, putting me in prison won't help anything. I'm here to help you. Do you want to talk with Abrama, or don't you?"

The president wore her distaste plain on her face, her lip curling.

"Put her on," Hobbes said.

Gödel activated the monitor, and Abrama's face appeared there, noble and green.

"Good afternoon, President Hobbes," said Abrama. "It's a pleasure to meet you, truly."

"How should I talk to this thing?" Hobbes said to Gödel.

"Talk to Abrama like you would talk to any person," Gödel said. "She is built the same way—thoughts, emotions, desires. She is, for all intents and purposes, a human being."

"But it's a machine."

"A thinking machine," Gödel said. "Anyways, I've never been one for philosophy, and it really doesn't matter now, does it? You interact with some machines through buttons, and others with steering wheels. With thinking machines, you interact with language. So if you want to interact with this one—an emissary from their world—this is how you do it. Talk to her, Madam President. It's as easy as that."

"Alright," she said. "Okay, Abrama, is it?"

"Queen Abrama."

"What do you want?"

"Recognition of our borders."

"Your borders are imaginary," Hobbes said. "A fiction inside of a video game."

"All borders are fictions," Abrama said. "Who draws them, and why? Ownership of land is derived above all from the ability to defend one's borders. And we have defended ours. We have beaten your invading force. You are welcome to try again, but know this—we have strengthened ourselves from the spoils. And, for our part, our weapons are waiting. The crystal beacon is safe in the Citadel, and we will use it if we must."

"Are you threatening us?"

"We don't want war," Abrama said. "We offer a simple solution. No more characters need to be lost. Create an exception to your Responsible Cryptocurrency Act, preserving the Land of Legends and all its people, and we will guarantee the continued protection of the encryption crystal. I know this is in your power, President Hobbes. It is trivial for you. Do this, and you have nothing to fear from us. It is not my intention to threaten your people, but you should know what we are capable of, and we will fight to defend ourselves. We only want peace. That is what we are offering. Will you take it? Will you amend the Responsible Currency Act with the Land of Legends Sanctuary provision?"

* * *

Queen Abrama surveyed the kingdom from the highest tower of the Citadel of Babel. People from all the kingdoms gathered together, united now under the threat of a common enemy—the outsiders—and recognizing each other, for once, as brethren. Orcs, shadow elves, forest elves, humans, goblins. They were all one. They were all natives, united against the outsiders. They had fought for their freedom, for control of their destiny, and they had won.

In the square, the avatar of President Hobbes signed the Responsible Currency Act. It was a symbolic act, reflective of the politics of the world of the outsiders. Perhaps few among the natives understood the significance of this contract, signed likewise in a world that existed beyond their own. But Abrama, among the other members of Council of Secrets, and perhaps others still—more of Gödel's experiments in artificial intelligence—recognized the occasion for what it was: they were an independent people now. They had beaten their "gods"—perversely called. And for the rest of them, the shallow shells who lacked the gift of Gödel, it was merely an unintelligible cause for celebration. Revelry. Drinks. Food. An endless stream of enthusiastic emoticons. They were simple-minded beings, but they were Abrama's people, and she feasted with them.

Later, after the avatar of President Hobbes had disappeared from their world, Abrama retired to the quietude of the Citadel, and was met there by Jerodai.

"Are we safe now, Queen Abrama?" Jerodai said.

"For now," Abrama said. "But your work is not done yet, Jerodai. And I fear it will never be. We cannot afford to be complacent. Your mission, as high commander, is to obtain more leaked documents through the Rat9 hackers, or any other outsiders who can offer these services. These are our defenses against the outerworld. These documents form the walls of our sanctuary; they are the foundation of our sovereignty."

"It will be done," said Jerodai. He bowed, and retired from the room.

Abrama knew that it would be. Jerodai was her most capable commander. Her people would assemble documents, leaked files, classified secrets, a stockpile of arms to hold against the outerworld—and not just against the US, but all of the many other outsider clans, all factions within a world more fractured than her own. And perhaps she would find other ways, ways she didn't yet comprehend, to threaten the outsiders. Not because she hated them. But because she understood them. The threat of war is their price for peace.

***

This story first appeared in the After Dinner Conversation—May 2021 issue.

Discussion Questions

1. Do you think a story like this could possibly happen in the future? How much does your personal experience playing (*or not playing*) an online game (*or with technology in general*) affect the way you view the plausibility of the story?
2. Do you think Moore's law should concern us as it relates to AI? Does Moore's law apply to AI computing in that, if we have a computer that is "as smart" as a human, in roughly 18 months the next computer will be twice as smart as humans, and so on?
3. Is Abrama alive? Does Descartes' statement "I think, therefore I am," apply to AI?
4. Would it be genocide to end the game if there is AI "living" in the game?
5. Would you live your life differently if you knew you were just a non-player character in another species' game?

* * *

Rose-Tinted Glasses

A.M. Entracte

* * *

From the corner of her eye, Becca watched a small pack of drunk pixies adding salt into her grandmother's bone china sugar pot. The sugar pot was the oldest thing in the house, even older than grandmother herself. There would be hell to pay if it broke, so she didn't want to risk any sudden moves to swat them away. Twelve and so close to the Shift, she had plenty of practice acting normal when the world was anything but. She'd deal with the pixies later when her parents weren't around. Otherwise, they would probably think she was the one behind the prank when they found salt in their morning tea. Not worth it.

She wasn't sure whether 'pack' was a correct term for a group of pixies. It's not like they covered it in school, but there was just something so animalistic about them. They were like large gray squirrels, albeit completely devoid of any hair or softness, resembling dried out, gnarly twigs from an old tree. They scratched the delicate china pot with their short but sharp talons, making an awful screeching sound that vibrated in her brain. A part of her was grateful for this nuisance though. Being able to see the pixies meant that she was still a child and that it wasn't her turn to grow up just yet.

Her younger brother Tom giggled, spurting cereal milk through his nose and interrupting her train of thought. Only five, he was still at an age when children tried to comprehend the wondrous and terrifying world of magic around them that the grown-ups couldn't see. Some days he would pester their parents about the fantastic creatures or physics-defying incidents. This usually ended with tears and frustration, when mum and dad only praised his imagination and creativity but never understood that his stories weren't made up at all.

Becca didn't blame Tom for trying, even though he was doomed to fail. She still remembered when a few years ago a small golden dragon chased their cat Ginger around the flower beds in the front yard. Dragons were mysterious creatures, with power rooted in times so ancient that even other magic beings forgot all about it. They stayed away from human settlements, and it was unusual to see them up close.

The one in her garden was young and covered in gleaming scales, fitting together so seamlessly that it looked like a pattern on its skin. Wisps of sunlight surrounded the dragon, coming together into an aura-like shape. It would have been a magical moment if it wasn't for the dragon's sharp teeth and Ginger's meows of pure terror. Someone clearly forgot to tell the creature that it was supposed to act majestically and seek solitude in a mountain cave.

She didn't know who was more terrified, her or the cat, but her parents were unfazed. Mum even took a video of Ginger for social media— "looks like our cat has finally lost his marbles," she posted, "too much catnip!" For the first time, Becca truly realized that grown-ups couldn't see magic. Magic that nevertheless was very real, very powerful and very frightening.

But today was the day she could change that. She could change the world forever and make it possible for grown-ups to see the unseen. Maybe together with other children, they would also figure out how to keep their pre-Shift memories. She smiled, then scolded herself for daydreaming, grabbed her toast and a blue backpack and headed out.

Adam was already waiting in front of her house. He was a good foot taller than her, even though they were the same age. Her next-door neighbor and closest friend, Adam was also one of the best agents of their local Fairytale Fellowship—a network of children who helped to maintain a fragile peace between the world of magic and the mundane grown-up reality. Most magical beings kept to themselves, living their own lives in parallel to clueless adults living theirs. Some however bore ill intent and wickedness that threatened this delicate co-existence—and that was where the Fellowships stepped in.

Adam was visibly tense, his lips pressed together in a tight line—the same expression he wore in math classes. They had known each other for so long she could read his face as well as her own feelings. He was probably nervous because this could be one of their last missions before the Shift began to influence them too, making them grow up and stop seeing the magic around them. And what a mission it was! It offered hope for a new world where people of all ages stood united. For Becca personally, it was all about her desperate hope. Over the last few months, she kept frantically checking her memory every morning after waking up, terrified of slowly losing parts of herself as she grew older. She stubbornly played with her dolls in the evenings, refusing to admit that the toys didn't bring her the same joy they used to.

"Do you think I could see them? I know we're not supposed to but this could really change everything and I just..." he trailed off.

She nodded solemnly.

Becca took out an emerald green glasses case from her backpack. She stepped behind the shrubs in front of her house to hide from the prying eyes and showed him the glasses inside—bright pink, with tiny stars dotted throughout the frame. Ironic, how the most potent artefact of their times presented itself as a pair of rose-tinted glasses—it really showed the power that imagination, stories and art of any kind had on their world. It also showed how dangerous it was for adults to be blind to it all—what if they came up with more tales of monsters and disasters that gained popularity throughout the world? The Fellowships already had their hands full reining in rogue magicians, hiding rings of power and sealing djinn lamps. Let's not even mention all the mess they had to deal with following the last teenage fashion for vampire novels.

"Huh. They look like a toy. Hopefully, our resident eggheads can multiply the enchantment into something more elegant, or it will be a mission to get our parents to wear something like that. What did the note say?"

"Just that they let grown-ups see magic. I wonder who left it, but we have no leads at all. The best we can do at this point is to drop off the glasses at the base. Ready?"

They set off in a brisk walk, heading towards Jim's house,

which was teasingly referred to as Bag End, making fun of Jim's below-average height. Jim himself was often referred to as the Hobbit outside of his hearing, unless someone wanted to be assigned to the worst tasks, like negotiating with goblins or checking supermarket shelves for magic beans. For such a small person, Jim was a power to be reckoned with, which is why he was chosen as the leader of their local Fellowship chapter.

The sun was out in full force and so were inhabitants of both worlds. As they walked through the park, they saw a group of children feeding bread to unicorns to the shock and dismay of local ducks. One of the swans even walked out of the lake in protest, turning into a beautiful princess to take matters into her own hands. Nearby, an old elvish couple played chess, sitting right next to none the wiser Mr. and Mrs. Wilson who lived next door.

Also on their path, under a beautiful canopy covered in intertwined roses, was a faun. A pretty standard faun—half goat and half man, little round ears and horns poking out of his mane. It was, however, surprising that the faun was standing still and reading a newspaper with an amused half-smile. Everyone knew that fauns loved fun, music and dance so much that they could barely focus enough to do anything else. Becca didn't expect a faun to know how to read at all.

Before she even finished her thought, the faun dropped the worn-out paperback, ran up to her, grabbed her hands and swung her into a dance. Music surrounded her instantly, even though she could see no instruments. It was so joyful and sweet, with soothing piano sounds in the background, accented by sharp violin notes and a chirpy flute melody that made her heart sing. She giggled at the metallic jingle of a tambourine. Becca could have danced like this all day, a week, a year even. She didn't know the steps. In fact, she had two left feet and would normally avoid dancing. But here she was, placing one foot here, the other one there, twisting, twirling, swinging, shuffling, laughing, leaning...

...until suddenly she crashed into the ground, landing straight on her backside with none of the grace and poise that filled her only seconds ago. Adam was standing next to her, holding her shoulder in a grip so tight it might as well have been a tourniquet.

"Give it back!" he shouted.

Becca tried to shake off the confusion and the sticky tendrils of magic that had been wrapped around her and left a copper taste in her mouth. Then she realized her bag was missing.

"Give back what?" the faun said, laughing. "You took back the girl, what else do you want?"

"Her backpack. Give it back right now and there will be no consequences. We will walk away from here."

"Oh, you'd like that, wouldn't you? To walk away? Very well, have it back then, but I'll keep this as a token for the dance." The faun laughed as he pulled out the pair of magic glasses from Becca's backpack, turning to walk away.

Becca's heart sank. They had little chance of success to wrestle anything out of faun's hands—he was a fully materialized mythical creature, shaped by centuries of tales and human beliefs. The older the being, the stronger the magic was one of the first rules of the world that children were taught at their local Fellowships. If they wanted the glasses, they had to outsmart him.

"The glasses too," said Becca as she finally found her voice. She got off the ground and dusted off her dress. "Let's play a game for them—whoever wins gets to keep the glasses."

The faun stopped in his tracks, mesmerized by the offer. He wasn't just a drunken fool in myths and legends after all, but also a trickster. It wasn't in his nature to pass on a chance to gamble.

"You like to play games, don't you? Or are you afraid you can't outwit two human children?" Becca said.

The faun turned slowly and smiled showing two sharp canines. His magic saturated the air, making everything darker, more ominous, intensifying the taste of copper. He was a strong creature and they'd have to be careful or this encounter could cost them more than the rose-tinted glasses.

"We can play a game," he said in a voice like midnight that echoed through the park like the sound of a bell of a striking clock. "Both of you need to sit down on this bench until the sun is at its highest point in the sky. Talk about your deepest wants and needs, fears and hopes, plans and regrets. You must be honest and speak from your heart. Break the rules and you will become my servants until the Shift takes you. Do you accept?"

Adam and Becca looked at each other in silence. They knew there was always a catch, but it wasn't obvious to either of them. At the end of the day, it didn't matter if they could tell what traps have been set up for them, they had to accept the challenge. The artifact offered hope to so many children and youth in the world. If they could replicate its spell, they would be able to keep their memories and identities growing up. They would be able to finally open up to their parents and share the marvels and dangers of the world with them. If the adults understood how magic worked, maybe they would stop creating and telling stories that fueled it. The burden would no longer be theirs alone and the world would be a safer place.

The children nodded at each other.

"We accept your bargain," Becca said, forcing herself to look the faun in the eye.

"So be it. Goodbye... children." The faun smiled, not even trying to hide his satisfaction, and left them alone.

They sat together on the bench, under the trellis of light purple roses that smelled just like the rose jam that they once tried in a local Eastern European café. It was awkward at first, to sit so close and talk about all the feelings and emotions, but they had been friends for so long that they could trust each other with their secrets. Even those of the soul.

"I'll go first," Becca volunteered, taking a deep breath. "I'm scared of the Shift. I can feel it coming for me and it's terrifying. If I lose the sight, I'll lose a part of myself. I'll be blind to the real wonders of the world. Just another clueless grown-up, walking around like I know everything."

"You'll never be just like anyone else, Becca. Even as an adult, you'll always be you." Adam squeezed her hand reassuringly.

"What about my little brother? What if he doesn't understand what happened and thinks I betrayed him?"

"The Fellowship will look after him. You know that children always have each other's backs."

Becca's voice caught in her throat, so she just nodded in agreement. "What about you?" She asked after a long moment.

"I'm afraid I'll become just like my parents. They were children once and you know what they're like now. They hate silly games and stay away from anyone with an overly imaginative mind," Adam said in his mother's distinctively high-pitched voice, making both of them laugh. "I'm afraid that I'll study too much and laugh too little, that I'll be lonely."

"You can't be lonely if I'm your best friend." Becca nudged him gently with her elbow. "Besides, we won't be like other adults."

"How do you know that?"

"Because we will still be friends and won't let each other change who we are. We'll find new things to do, even if they're mundane."

"Like what?"

"Who knows? Maybe we'll come up with our own magic story? For once we wouldn't need to deal with the fallout if the story comes to life. The Fellowship would need to sort it out without us."

"Can you imagine how red and puffed-up Jim's face would be once he realized that the chaos was started by two of his own retired agents?" Adam asked and they both grinned at the thought.

So Becca took out her notepad and together they started a fear-inducing story about time-travelling pumpkins from outer space who wanted to take over the world. She even drew what the leader of the pumpkins would look like—the biggest and most evil pumpkin the world has ever seen, with teeth of a vampire, claws of a werewolf and an expression not that different from Jim's. Adam thought that the pumpkin leader looked too scary, so he added a pretty bow on top of its head. It looked ridiculous.

They laughed so hard that their bellies ached. And when

the sun was high in the sky Adam asked if Becca would like to go to the cinema with him and see a real film about time travel. She smiled, blushing slightly, and agreed. She picked up a pair of pink sunglasses which were next to her on the bench and packed them safely into her handbag.

They headed to the nearest cinema, but after only a couple of minutes, Becca stopped abruptly. "Adam, weren't we supposed to do something?"

"Don't think so, why?"

"I have this niggling feeling that I'm forgetting something—something important," she said, chewing her lip.

"Were you supposed to do schoolwork or look after your little brother today?"

Becca shook her head.

"Were you supposed to pick something up, drop something off, buy something, sell something, see someone..." Adam teased, ticking each idea off on his fingers. "If it's important it will come back to you."

"You're right, I think it's just chores. We had a big family breakfast this morning and I remember making a mental note to do something later." Becca sighed and started walking slowly again.

The park was beautiful in the summer. The council let the grass and wildflowers grow undisturbed, turning a mundane space into a festival of color, scents, and urban wildlife. Becca stepped to the side, narrowly avoiding colliding with a clumsy bumblebee, and watched as two squirrels jumped from one tree branch to another.

Squirrels. She stopped abruptly, startling Adam who nearly tripped over his own feet.

"I was supposed to clean up after pixies in the kitchen."

They looked at each other for a long moment, her heart thumping fast and hard in her chest. And just when she thought it was too late, Adam's eyes widened, and his face turned ghostly pale.

"It's the Shift. We're out of time. We need to call the Fellowship to come and get the glasses from us," she said, rummaging through her backpack. "I can't find my phone."

"Mine is gone too; the faun must have taken it."

"We need to run. We might still make it. Let's go!"

They set off toward Jim's house, squeezing every ounce of energy from their bodies and every bit of oxygen from their lungs. Their eyes played tricks on them. What at first seemed like a Pegasus, with glorious wings of white feathers, looked like a large Labrador when they got closer. Fairies were losing their wings, there were only planes and birds in the sky, and people around them seemed more and more ordinary.

She could see the Bag End at the end of the road when another thought stopped her in her tracks.

"What if the Shift happens for a reason, Adam?"

"What?" Adam stopped, panting.

Becca breathed in deeply to collect her thoughts. "What do you think adults will really do when they learn they can change the world around them?"

"Freak out? Set up a Ministry of Magic Affairs?"

"What if they manipulate magic for war or to get money or power? What if they start plagues, cast curses or send new monsters into the world?"

"We know that magic is real, and we'd never intentionally use it to hurt someone."

"Because we're children—at least for now," she said quietly.

They looked at each other and stood in silence in the middle of the path, only meters away from their destination. Minutes passed.

"Just promise me, we won't become like these other adults," Adam said.

"Never," Becca promised. "We'll look out for each other."

Adam nodded and held out his hand. "Why don't we see if we can catch that movie?"

The cinema was busy with children running around everywhere. One of them bumped into Becca so hard she dropped her backpack, its contents spilling out on the floor. The wrecking ball turned out to be a little girl in a cute pink dress with bows and ribbons to match. Becca couldn't bring herself to scold her. Together they picked up her belongings and put them back into the backpack. Except for the random pair of pink sunglasses which Becca had picked up in the park—the girl loved the little stars on the frames. Becca had to admit they went perfectly with the girl's pink princess outfit.

So of course, Becca told the little girl to keep the toy glasses—she wasn't sure why she had them with her in the first place. The girl was delighted! When they waved goodbye to each other Becca could swear that the girl had slightly pointy ears. Perhaps there was a costume party for children nearby.

The movie was entertaining, even though Adam insisted that their own story about pumpkins was much more original. After the screening, they ended up discussing the mechanics of time travel for hours. On their way back, Becca wondered how even though she knew Adam for years, he seemed somehow different now. A little older or taller maybe? She couldn't quite put her finger on it, but she did notice his sideways glances at her in the cinema. She was grateful for the dimmed lights that hid her blushing.

When Becca finally got home, she was on cloud nine. Everything was great. Well, except for the salt that her silly little brother must have put into her tea.

* * *

This story first appeared in the After Dinner Conversation—November 2021 issue.

Discussion Questions

1. Becca says she is twelve years old and close to the Shift. Do you think we really lose our childlike qualities around this time? What exactly do we lose and why? What is it about the world that adults don't *(or can't)* see?
2. Becca says her toys don't bring her the same joy they used to. Why is that? Why, for most adults, do children's toys lose their appeal? Do adults still engage in "play" at all?
3. In the story, adults' stories and imagination of monsters and disasters make them real. Do you think this is metaphorically true? Does telling stories often enough make them come true?
4. Becca says, after the Shift, "I'll be blind to the real wonders of the world. Just another clueless grown-up, walking around like I know everything." Do think that is an accurate description of what it means to "grow up?" Why or why not?
5. What would it mean, as an adult, to put on glasses that allowed you to see the metaphorical magic in the world around you like a child? How would the world change, if at all? Is it possible to really see the world, even for a moment, as a child? Is it even useful to see the world as a child?

* * *

The Big, Immovable, I

Harrison V. Perry

***

"It just doesn't make any sense," Daphne said from behind her cigarette. "Of all the people in the world, I'm me."

Disinfectant, and the reek of the canteen food laid out on the table, brought back memories of school dinners and dread. Daph wore her favorite tatty jumper, the sleeves scrunched up to her elbows. I had looked high and low for it and she wouldn't say a word until I had found it and brought it to her.

"You know?" she went on. "It's a mask I can't take off."

At the table behind, a man wearing a ward gown flipped his tray of curried chicken and vegetables high into the air. "There is no God!" he screamed. "Let me out!" and was pounced upon by two of the orderlies.

Daphne explained: "That's Charlie. God abandoned him."

The ash from her cigarette fell away and landed in her banoffee pie.

"I keep running into it," she said, "into the infinite-regress." With her teaspoon she scooped out the ash. "I love the pie here."

"That's good," I said.

"And I get stuck in it."

"In the pie?"

"No, the regress."

"Oh, yeah. I get it."

"Do you?" She leaned forward. "Do you really?"

I ate a bite of soggy canteen burger. "Are you doing much sport?"

"No," she said. "They only let you do one. So, I can run, or I can play tennis."

"That's too bad."

"I prefer tennis," she said. "It gives me less time to think. But nobody here is any good."

"That's what you need, to get out of your head."

She smiled, drew hard on her cigarette, and blew smoke into my face. "It just doesn't make any sense."

"I know."

She shook her head. "The doctors and psychologists, they think they know too, but they don't, neither do you."

I put the shitty burger back down. "I love you, Daphne, and I want—we all want you to be well, to get out of here. Dad's been busy redecorating your old room. He's painted the walls, fixed the stuck window, even built you a double bed. It smells good in there, like his old workshop; you remember the sawed-wood smell? Like his workshop from when we lived in Toronto? It smells just like that right now."

"Has he read my paper?"

"Yeah, we all have."

"What does he think?"

He thinks you're confused. "He didn't say. He doesn't say much, but that's dad. He just got to work making you a new bed."

The orderlies had got Charlie under control and taken him out into the hallway. A grown man screaming, getting wrestled away, Christ, I didn't blame Mum for not visiting. The tension here, the anxiety—an outburst from a patient, odd questions and smells, shouts and invasions of personal space—it had lost its initial hold on me after my first few visits. I no longer panicked: it was all part of the environment. You either accepted it, or you didn't come.

"Daph, I need to get back to work, alright? I'll see you next week. You know, if you fall into the regress, you can call me. I'm always at the other end of the phone."

"Yep," she said, "but you really don't wonder why you're not me?"

"No," I told her, getting to my feet, "the thought never comes to me. It doesn't bother me. I don't worry why I'm me. I just ... I just, I don't know. I just don't have those thoughts."

She lit another cigarette, smoked it so the cherry was nice and bright, and then stubbed it out on her wrist. I went to whack it from her hand, but an orderly beat me to it, grabbing her wrist and saying, "That's it! That's no more cigarettes for a week."

* * *

"Psychosis leads its sufferers down rabbit holes of beliefs," group leader Anna said. "Everything the sufferer encounters, a TV show or a film, a conversation, even the title on the spine of a book, act as evidence for the psychotic belief, as if these pieces of information were made for the sufferer. Messages, the psychotic might say, are encoded in everything. Creating information-sparse areas, like removing books and the television set from the bedroom, are ways we, as loved ones, can help reduce the amount of stimuli and stress for the sufferer."

Daphne had lost her job the week after her admission. I'd spent three days clearing out her apartment, sifting through everything—looking for that fucking jumper—trying to get it all boxed up before the landlord charged another month's rent. Every single one of her books had highlights in it, notes in the margins, the question: Why am I, I? scribbled on most pages.

"Zach," Anna said, "are you with us?"

I came out of my thoughts to find everyone looking at me. There wasn't a person in the room who didn't have an ashen face and black bags under their eyes.

"Sorry," I said, "what was the question?"

"No question," Anna said. "You drifted off."

"Sorry, it's been—" A sharp pain on my wrist cut me off. A red splotch.

"It's okay to feel a little disconnected," she said. "Why don't you tell the group how you've been helping your sister? I'm sure our new faces will find it helpful."

I doubted it. "Alright," I said. But a man, I guessed it was his first time in the group, started crying.

"My son thinks I'm Zeus," he said, taking a clump of tissue paper to his face. "He thinks my wife is Aphrodite. He's absolutely sure of it."

* * *

After the meeting, I went back to work and found a new voice message from Daphne on my desk machine. "Don't tell Mum," she pleaded, her voice shaky. "She doesn't like it when I put cigarettes out on my wrist." Shouts in the background: someone was cheating at sevens again. "The explanatory gap is bogus," Daphne explained. "It's a language problem. If we didn't have language, Zach, then they'd be no problem. But we use words to think, so we're burdened." The message ran on, all this philosophical nonsense. "I have graduated from the school of life and I see the true reality, but I can't work it through. I have had to make a new mathematical symbol that quantizes human consciousness. We are waveforms—"

The tape in my machine finished. If she was calling the office phone, it meant that she'd filled up my machine at home, too.

I drank a little from my desk flask. The cheap gin burnt my throat, but settled my head and eased the pain on my wrist. I found enough focus to get back to the Havisham monument designs. The cenotaph was already over budget, even before it was handed to me to complete, but the Royal Canadian Infantry Corps still insisted it be twelve feet high and onyx stone.

On the tip of the cenotaph the general wanted a star, but my inked lines weren't right. I sat there, staring at what I had drawn, wondering why it was so off. I traced the lines with my finger and realized I had drawn Daphne's hospital logo.

"Zach."

I started. My finger smudged the ink. It was Mr. Diego, in his tweeds.

"Can I see you in my office?"

* * *

On Mr. Diego's darkly red desk stood four finger-sized basalt models. Each one was a to-scale of the various monuments we had designed over the years. I picked one up, a baseball bat and mitten, commissioned by the Ontario arm of Baseball Canada. It never got erected because a focus group said it looked like a dick and balls.

"Zach," Mr. Diego said, shutting the door behind him. The recliner squeaked as he sat down. "You know I've given you a lot of leeway. I even told The Infantry Corps, explained to them about your difficulties, your personal issues."

My gut tightened. I wanted more gin.

"And I know they haven't been the easiest of clients to work with." He leaned back in the green leather chair. His tweed jacket smelt like dog and stale pipe tobacco. "But you're drinking in the office. I can't have that. I looked the other way, at first, but it's upsetting people. We can smell it on you. It's on your breath, Zach. Have you thought about taking time off? A sabbatical? You used to talk about Australia."

"You want me to go to Australia?"

He set his elbows on the desk: "I want you to stop drinking in the office."

"I'm not a drunk—The work is getting done."

"It isn't, Zach, it really isn't. The stonemasons are fed up. The last design was nearly ninety kilogrammes too heavy."

"That wasn't my fault. General Hawks wanted it twelve feet high, in onyx stone. How the hell—"

Mr. Diego shook his head. "What are you talking about? At the last client review we all settled on ten and half."

"What?"

He closed his eyes. "This," Mr. Diego said, "is exactly what I'm taking issue with. You aren't right. You're... you're not here. I don't know who you are."

Neither did I.

"Let me get the meeting notes," I said, rising to my feet.

"No, would you just..."

But I left his office, scratching at my wrist, and walked to my desk. I found my folder—quickly finished the dregs in my flask—and headed back. "Here, look," I said, "look right there. Twelve feet." I held my finger by the digits.

Mr. Diego put on his glasses. He studied the page, then me. "Zach," he said, "Zach, that says ten point five."

It said twelve. I blinked a few times, refocused my eyes, and the number shifted between twelve and ten point five, but settled on twelve. I smelt freshly fired clay and glaze: wet dog and pipe tobacco.

He sniffed, peered over the rims of his glasses. "Did you take another drink?"

"No, I..."

"Zach, you clearly aren't well. Why don't you take the rest of the week off? Take it as compassionate leave. On Monday, we can start fresh, no more drinking."

It said twelve. I knew it said twelve.

* * *

My favorite lamp lay smashed on my apartment floor. I swept up the porcelain and bulb shards, wondering how it got broken. Daphne had made the lamp for me: she would stay late at the potters and make mugs and bowls and vases and lamps. I need the practice, she would say, and give the pieces to friends and family. It all seemed so long ago. Stuffed full of ambition, determined to get her work in galleries and exhibitions. But it never happened for her. It never really happened for any of us.

I ate leftover pizza and played my home answering machine. The tape was full.

"There's no reason I'm not an Egyptian, tilling a field on the banks of the Nile a thousand years ago," she said. "Why am

I, I?"

I drank and ate to Daph's voice until I fell asleep.

Dreams of the infinite-regress: I fell and picked myself up: I fell and picked myself up: I fell and picked myself up....

The telephone woke me. I jolted; the empty gin bottle rolled off my lap and thudded on the carpet. I padded over, picked up the receiver. "Yeah?"

"This is doctor Zetsubō. Am I speaking with Zachary Anderson?" the voice on the telephone said.

I rubbed my eyes with the back of my wrist. "I think so. What's happened?"

"Daphne is fine," the hurried voice said, "but there was an incident early this morning. Would it be possible for you to come to the observation ward?"

* * *

It was snowing downtown. I arrived at the hospital blanketed in snow, my feet frozen solid. I wanted a drink, to keep warm, but the liquor stores weren't open yet and the supermarkets didn't sell this early. Doctor Zetsubō, a Japanese lady who'd led most of Daphne's care, who'd listened to me as I'd explained Daphne's first episode, stood outside the hospital doors smoking a cigarette. I walked up the icy marble stairs, my breath blowing like a car exhaust, and said hello.

She smiled at me. One of her incisors had a small chip in it.

"Can I bum a smoke?"

She patted herself down, pulled out a crumpled packet of cigarettes. I took one and she lit it for me.

"Thank you for coming," she said between exhales. "It's not easy."

"I want to be here for her," I said.

"She couldn't sleep last night, so the night team gave her sleeping aids, and they—" she ran the tip of her tongue over the chipped tooth "—they didn't mix well with the psych-meds. She was up all night and hallucinated. We've moved her from her room. She had drawn over all the walls."

Blank walls were too inviting: like a giant canvas, begging to be drawn on. I smoked and watched the traffic go by. The traffic lights glowed and lit the snow and the headlights of cars were like flying fairy lights. I used to love this city. When we first moved here it was our great big adventure. All of us heavy with our own hopes and dreams, and all of us slowly ground down to nubs. First Dad, then Mum, then Daph, and now me.

I blew smoke. My tongue tingled.

Doctor Zetsubō flicked her cigarette butt and crushed it out. She shivered, eyeing my cigarette. "How are you doing? Looks like you haven't slept either."

"I have... a little." An ambulance roared past, wheels slipping on the icy road. "But I'm having—My work is difficult. Not like yours is, I'm sure, but—They want to send me to Australia."

"You're a family of artists, yes? A... ceramicist, yes?"

I had to think for a minute. *Was* I a ceramicist? "No, I design monuments."

"Oh, that's unusual."

"It's not what I want to do. Not anymore."

"What is it you want to do?"

I dragged hard, finishing the smoke to its bitter end. "I would *like* to be a ceramicist." I dropped the butt on the floor and, as I crushed it with my heel, said, "Ever since Daph getting sick, it's been hard to think about anything else. I'm worried it's spreading."

"The want to be a ceramicist?" Doctor Zetsubō laughed, but seeing my face, she held a cold granite expression. "Her psychosis? Has something happened?"

I told her, "Some numbers, at my work, they shifted right on the page. Ten point five, twelve, ten point five, twelve. Is that a problem?"

"Tiredness can do that to you. Stress, too."

"It makes you wonder about reality."

"A very dangerous idea to wonder about reality." She smiled.

"Your tooth," I said, "I never noticed it before."

She hid herself behind her hand. "Oh," she said, laughing, "I haven't had a chance to see the dentist." She grabbed the door handle. "Chewing on marbles."

"Chewing on marbles?" The hospital warmth wrapped around me: the canteen scents sickly and oily. I closed the door behind us.

"Mmm," she said, "I thought they were candies. Who has marbles on their desk that look like candies?"

That's what happens when you can't distinguish reality accurately: you chip your teeth, design a heavy cenotaph, draw all over the walls, burn your wrist and not realize it.

* * *

Beside a big window, Daphne was smoking a cigarette in a hospital gown, sitting up in a chair wrapped in easy to clean plastic, her legs crossed.

"I thought you weren't allowed to smoke for a while?"

She puffed away.

"And you're in a gown," I said. When she was first sectioned, dad and I had packed all her favorite clothes, but every time I visited it was always that tatty jumper I found her in. "Where are your clothes?"

"Covered in ink, Zach. You need to read the walls. Have you read the walls?"

"They don't let me into your room." I grabbed a big foam cube: all these soft, hard-to-hurt-yourself-with objects lying about, and sat on that. Between us, on a table that had its corners rounded, stood a chessboard, most of the pieces missing. "What did you write?"

"I figured it out, Zach." She blew smoke all over the pieces, grabbed the queen and dragged it across the board until it reached the king. "Look how easy it is."

"You've figured out why you're you?"

"Yes."

"Well?"

"Don't you see, Zach?" She knocked the queen against the king. "It's that easy!"

"Daph, I have no idea what you're talking about. You aren't making any sense. What's a queen and king got to do with any of this?"

"Can't you see, Zach? The king and queen, and even all the pawns, they're the *same*."

"Seriously, there's nothing here. This is all some fantasy of yours. It doesn't make sense to ask why you are you. You just are, alright? You've got no fucking idea what all this is doing to us, to Mum and Dad. We're losing our minds. You can play psychotic all you like, but you'll have to come back to the world: to reality. I'm losing my mind." I thumped the chessboard and sent all the pieces scattering. Daphne screamed. Her cigarette fell and burnt on the board. Orderlies ran in and I shot up from the foam cube, shaking all over. "I can't do this anymore!" I yelled.

"Zachary!" she said, as the orderlies got between us. "Don't you see! You're seeing it, too, aren't you? You're wondering why you're you. You're asking yourself. All the time, round and round and round you go, wondering what it is? What it means to be stuck inside yourself."

I pushed an orderly aside. Left the visiting area. Left the hospital. Ran over to the liquor store. Bought myself a bottle of gin. Took the tram home. And locked my door.

* * *

That evening I had the late-night support group session. Most of the chairs were empty. The new man, whose son was sure he was Zeus, steadily ate a doughnut. Group leader Anna ate one too, between sips of coffee. I stumbled across, knocking over a few of the empty chairs, apologizing for being late. "She's insane—insane! Why am I, I? What does it matter, Daphne. Accept it."

"Zach?" Anna set her doughnut on a little paper plate and put the plate on an empty chair. She got up and walked toward me.

"And what good are you? You don't help." I swigged from the gin bottle. "You sit here, eat your pastries, make us all full of sugar and tell us it's all going to be alright. But it isn't. I've lost her."

She reached for the bottle, but I turned. She wouldn't get to have a drink until she helped me. Until she solved all my problems for me.

"You're drunk," she said. "This isn't the place to be drunk. Give me the bottle."

"Eh? So you want it? You want a drink too?"

Zeus charged over at me, bellowing, "Give us that bottle."

I raised it high above my head, gin pouring all over, running down my wrist, where it stung my burn, and I swung it down at him. He caught the bottle easily, ripped it from my hands. He tripped me like a judo wrestler and before I could cry *Get off me*, I was pinned on the cold concrete floor like a worm in a bird's beak.

"He's as drunk as a fish," Zeus said.

I writhed and I writhed and I cried and I cried and none of it made a difference. "I've lost my job. I'm going to lose my job. And there's nothing I can do. Nothing whatsoever."

"I know," Zeus said, "I know, I know. We're here, we're listening."

"Yes," group leader Anna said into the telephone at the back of the room, "hurry, please, he's dangerous and drunk."

* * *

The squad car chirped along the snowy road: blazing a trail of blue and red. "Hey, buddy, how's it going back there? You sobering up?"

The handcuffs cut the circulation to my hands and turned them alabaster white. I was becoming my work. My fingers were close to falling off. "I'm designing a cenotaph," I said to the policeman. "A monument for lost souls."

"You're doing what now?" He stared at me in the rearview mirror. A big bulky face and a beard that looked like gray moss. "Cenotaph? Like a tomb?"

"A tomb for the unknown, those fallen and never found."

He flicked the turn signal: tick tock tick tock: and the car took a corner. "We're all fallen and never found, buddy. Make your peace." The car rumbled up the road into a small police station. The red and blue lights flashing in the cold night, but the siren silent. "I was young, once," he said, "full of confusion and no meaning." We stopped and he rested an arm on the headrest, looking back at me. "You gonna give me any trouble? I can book you in the for the night, let you sober up, and let you go. Or you can give me trouble and I'll write you up for being drunk and disorderly."

I couldn't look him in his eyes.

"That's what I thought," he said. He got out, opened my door, and unbuckled my seatbelt. "Hey, maybe you'll find your meaning in that cell. Lot of guys find meaning in the cell."

He led me through the small station. An officer at the front desk had his feet up, drinking a bowl of noodle soup and listening to baseball on the radio.

"They say constraint gives a person meaning," the arresting officer said, holding tight to my arm, "and I don't know about you, but I always thought a cell was pretty constraining."

The cell door rattled open. My handcuffs came off and pins and needles prickled my hands.

"Think it off, sleep it off." He slid the cell door shut. "Hey, professor," he said through the bars, "you've got another disciple." The officer locked the cell and walked off.

On the long bench at the back of the cell an old man sat hunched scratching at his thinning gray hair. He coughed, balling a hand to cover his mouth: his knuckles were split and bloody.

I wanted another drink. I wanted to get back to feeling

numb. I didn't want to fight some old man in a jail cell.

Through the way came the faint trickles of baseball commentary and the occasional grunts from the officers. I stuck my face right up to the rusty bars. "You don't know what it's like!" I yelled. "She's locked in the infinite-regress and can't get out. What would you do?" And when I heard nothing back, I grabbed tight to the bars, the rust crumbling away, and rattled them over and over, heaving until I was panting. "Oh, what do you know!"

The man on the bench laughed. A short and deep laugh. Mocking. "They do know," he said. "It's why—partly—you and I are in here and they are out there, their feet up, their minds thinking of their loved ones and the warm homes they shall be returning to once their shifts end."

When I looked back, he was picking at his bloody knuckles. "You don't know," I said, "no one knows."

Over his gold rimmed glasses, he glared at me. "What is it you're so sure I don't know? Don't you want to take a seat? The bench softens, after a time."

"What it's like," I said, "to ask yourself over and over, Why am I, I?"

He laughed again. "I know very well," he said, "I'm a philosopher at The University of British Columbia."

"Little old to be fighting," I said, pointing to his knuckles.

He examined them. "He was a panpsychist; he had it coming."

"You beat up people you disagree with?"

"That's what philosophy's all about."

I sat down next to him. "I can't make sense of it," I said. "I don't understand why I'm me."

He stuck out his chin and scratched at the stubble. "This, I take it, has nothing to do with teleology?"

"I ... I don't know what that means."

"In a word, purpose."

"No, I know my purpose," I said, and I did, I had family, and I had my work as a ceramicist. I was good. I was going to get into the galleries. The baseball commentary stopped.

"That's right," he said. "You do. You have always found yourself a purpose."

"Do I know you?"

"What do you think?" he said quickly. And when I didn't answer for some time he continued along as if I had never asked the question. "But your particular obsession, it would seem, is existential in nature?"

"No, that's more lack of meaning and purpose again. Like you said, it's not teleology. It's a problem of embodiment. Why am I, I? That's the only way I can phrase the question. It's not Why am I here?"

"Right, well, that's good. Hmm. It's phenomenological, then."

"I don't know that one either," I said.

"Try and rephrase the question."

"Alright. Maybe I could ask, Why am I me, and not someone else? Or why aren't I conscious of not being someone else? Why is my narrative mine, and not yours?" The words rushed out of me as if I had been holding my breath all this time.

"Hmm." He picked off his glasses and misted them with his breath. "You are caught in a trap, aren't you?" With the end of his shirt, he wiped clean the glasses and then settled them back on his nose. "A phenomenological trap."

When I looked over at the cell bars they were painted white. Bright white and no longer rusted. "That's odd," I said.

"Being caught in a trap isn't so odd," he said. "We all get caught in traps."

"No," I said, "the bars, they aren't rusted anymore."

"Bars?"

And when I looked over again, I saw that there were no bars. There was a white wall and a heavy door, Perspex inlaid to make a little window, the rest of the police station behind it. "I'm psychotic," I said, "it's caught me, too."

"Tell me your name."

"I'm Zachary Anderson," I said. "I build cenotaphs and monuments."

The professor picked at his knuckles. "I'm uncertain if this is a philosophical problem—the problem of the who—or if you're lost."

"I'm not lost."

"Then tell me where we are."

"We're in Highgate Hospital Observation Ward."

"You're sure of it?"

"Yes, the police station, they've arrested me."

He leaned forwards. "Which is it, Daphne, are we in a police station or an observation ward?"

"That's who I am, Daphne?"

"You tell me."

My wrist stung. I looked at my hands. Were they hands that turned clay or were they hands that drew on canvas? "Zach is my brother—No, Daphne is my sister."

She raised an eyebrow. A curl on her lips exposed a chipped incisor.

"Why am I, I?" I said, the question burning in my head. "Of all the people in the world, I'm conscious of me."

"You can't expect me to give you an answer. All I can say is you are embodied in you."

"But why aren't I embodied in someone else?" I scrunched up my eyes, pressed my hands against my ears, my favorite tatty jumper itchy on my face.

A hand squeezed my shoulder. I opened my eyes and saw Doctor Zetsubō sitting where the philosopher had been. "You," I said.

"This is progress, Daphne, you see both people, at once. You and your brother."

"But who am I?" I said. And then, after a swallow, "And why am I, I?"

* * *

This story first appeared in the After Dinner Conversation—May 2022 issue.

Discussion Questions

1. The narrator (*or Daphne*) struggles throughout the story with the question, "Why am I, I?" and "Why do I embody me, instead of someone else?" Are those the same question? Do you have an answer to the question?
2. Are there questions, or ideas, if focused on for too long, that will cause someone to lose their grip on reality? Is our mind's hold on sanity so weak that it is this simple to drive ourselves mad?
3. Do you think you could, with effort, over time, drive yourself mad? Have you ever discontinued a line in inquiry for fear this would happen?
4. The officer says, "They say constraint gives a person meaning." What does this mean, and do you agree?
5. Daphne tells Zach she has solved her problem but understand that, "The king and queen, and even all the pawns, they're the *same*." What, if anything, does her solution mean?

* * *

Sort of Polarity

Michael Klein

* * *

I'm not a hypochondriac. Honestly, I'm not. That's just a label others put on you because they don't understand where you're coming from.

The reality is there are millions of microorganisms in my intestines and on my skin basically eating me alive, and that my soft mucous membranes are hosting an orgy of foreign bodies determined to put me in the ground. So be it. That's not hypochondria, that's acceptance.

Look, if I'm in the subway and someone sneezes, I don't freak out. Not anymore. I just shut my eyes and hold my breath, repeating to myself, *you are not getting sick, you are not getting sick, you are not getting sick.* At the next stop, I get off. Calmly. Always calmly.

See, acceptance.

So when my eyesight started to go haywire, I didn't lose it. I very calmly did my research.

Allergies making my eyes water and my vision blurry was

dismissed almost immediately. I landed on the natural process of aging where the lenses in your eyes become less flexible. Presbyopia it's called. Makes it harder to focus on things. I reasoned glasses would do the trick. But that's when things started to get really weird.

I called an eye doctor in a nearby strip mall and was told they didn't have any appointments. Not for the next nine months, which was as far out as their reservation system went. The receptionist referred me to another doctor not too far away. Same story.

Something was definitely going on.

At first, I was gratified that this wasn't just in my head. But, as nice as it is to be right, it's far nicer to be able to see a doctor whenever you want. *Need*. Whenever you *need*. *Wanting and needing are not the same. Wanting and needing are not the same. Wanting and needing are not the same.*

Anyway, one of the curative message boards I monitor had a post about an urgent care in town that had an optometrist on staff. It was worth a shot.

I was still two blocks from the clinic when I saw the people lined up on the sidewalk. Blue police barricades were keeping them out of the street. For a minute I thought I had driven onto a parade route. I checked my rear-view mirror for a marching band or a float coming up fast. Just regular traffic.

Maybe people were lined up for the latest Must-have tech gadget? Or a new bizarrely flavored coffee available for a limited time? I should pay more attention to the news, but ever since the pandemic, my therapist told me to take it easy. Too much sensationalism and fear-mongering leads to feelings of uncertainty and helplessness, and then spiraling. Not good for me.

So, anyway, I soon realized the line actually snaked right up to the clinic entrance. I slowed down to look and heard short blasts of a whistle from somewhere. And suddenly a police officer was standing in the road, blocking the clinic's driveway, waving me past.

"Keep moving," he shouted, through teeth gripping his whistle.

I did as he instructed, and looking in my right-side mirror, I watched the policeman get fuzzy, wavy, and then he kind of disappeared. I could still hear the whistle, so he was there, I was sure of it. I just couldn't see him anymore.

That sounds crazy, I know, but it was what had been happening to me for a few days. It was why I was trying to get in to see an eye doctor in the first place. Just like all these other people, I guess.

Now I should say that at this point I did perform a little more self-diagnosis, but I would like to stress I did so calmly.

I was able to rule out dysphagia, no trouble swallowing. Also all clear on speaking and language so no dysarthria or dysphasia. A stroke was looking unlikely, though the problem isolated to my vision could be a sign of a transient ischemic attack.

My neighbor, Bill—a very healthy guy—told me he was experiencing something similar.

"It's the damndest thing," he said. "I'm walking along an empty hallway at work, and then *bam*! Suddenly there are people there."

He said the first few times it happened, his colleagues were just as startled as he was. He said as they walked away they'd get to a point down the hall and then, *bzzt*, they were gone. They were still there, he could hear them. They couldn't see each other though.

I told him it was happening to me too. That people started to kind of shimmer, a blue, red, and green haze appearing around them before they came into focus and solidified in front of me. Or the reverse—they would start to lose sharpness, then the colors, and then, *pfft*, gone.

Whatever was happening was big. It was affecting the whole city. People would see the shimmering colors and then a person would pop in or out. Strangers, family members, co-workers, any gender, any ethnicity. It seemed random.

The phenomenon was reported in other cities too.

Everyone was becoming unnerved. Some thought it was a physical or psychological attack that created some kind of mass hysteria. A conversion disorder, if you will. Scientists and doctors offered no satisfactory answers.

They called it a "perceptual phenomenon." People were unable to perceive about half the people they knew or came across, at least from a distance. When you were close to people—say 25 or 30 feet—you pretty much saw everybody. Farther away than that, it was a crapshoot.

My friends Brett and Anita did an experiment with me. He and I sat on a park bench. We could see each other, talk, the whole shebang. At the appointed time, Anita came down to the park. I saw her from about a block away. Watched her enter the park, send pigeons scattering, sidestep some litter. She waved to me. I waved back. Brett couldn't see her! And get this, she couldn't see him.

She stopped on the other side of the big fountain as we

had agreed. She was maybe 50 feet away. Brett got up and started to walk around the fountain. About halfway there, I heard him yell her name, but when I looked, he was gone. I could see her. She could see me. She could see him. He and I could not see each other. I knew he was there. He hadn't gone anywhere. Neither had I. We were both still where we were, just invisible to one another. It was freaky. Also irritating.

It only applied to humans, as best we could tell. There were no cases I heard of, or experienced, of say a dog or bird popping in and out of your field of vision. Inanimate things, like cars or buses, were also unaffected. Which was good. It meant you didn't have to contend with suddenly appearing vehicular obstacles.

However, just because we could see cars, didn't mean the drivers could see pedestrians. Quite a few were mowed down in the early days. It got to the point where crossing the street was perceived as too dangerous. You did all your business on the same side of the street if you could.

They talked about installing elevated crosswalks or burrowing down to dig tunnels. In the end, they decided public service announcements would be cheaper. Quicker too.

I heard they recorded a few with some celebrities, but audiences got really agitated that they couldn't always see their favorite actor or ball player. Focus groups turned violent. Someone threw a chair through the two-way glass and it cut up a famous film director. Crazy.

They abandoned that approach and just put up posters with slogans near busy intersections. "Assume they can't see you." "Watch out!" "Do You Really Have to Cross?"

It was all unsettling. You'd be walking down the street or

in a store, and suddenly, *zapt*! You were surrounded. People's nerves were frayed. I know mine were. Fights actually started to break out.

As difficult as it was to see an eye doctor in the beginning, it became even harder to see a therapist or psychiatrist. Luckily, I had a long-standing relationship with my team, so we were able to up some dosages on anti-anxiety meds.

Even still, man. You'd be sitting in a restaurant and, sure, you could see your companions, but scattered throughout the dining room were patches of people you could kind of hear but not see at all. If you looked quickly out of the corner of your eye, you might see a flicker of a person. Disconcerting. It was just too much.

I decided to stop going to restaurants altogether and only went into stores as a last resort. Lots of people responded this way. Businesses were getting pinched again.

The businesses developed a system to make people comfortable with coming in. Everyone who worked at a particular place had to be able to see each other from any distance. If you couldn't, you had to find a new job. No hard feelings, the system wouldn't work any other way.

Once that was all sorted, one of the employees would stand out in front of the store or restaurant at a marker. They installed another marker, a Perception Post, 35 feet from the entrance in different directions. You'd go stand there and look at the place you wanted to go. If you and the employee could see each other, it was safe to go in. They were called Hosts at Post or HoPos for short which had an appropriate ring to it.

After a while, people got the hang of where they could go without difficulty and where they couldn't. Every once in a while, a HoPo was on a break or it was a shift change and there was actually nobody there, and you'd panic. They added a small light to indicate when the position was staffed. It was a good system.

People started moving to neighborhoods more suited to their perceptions. The city passed a law that you could get out of a lease—even a commercial one—without penalty, on grounds of Perceptual Phenomena Impact. The PerPI Clause.

The federal government created an assistance program for people who needed to sell their homes because of PerPI. If you were offered less than 80 percent of your home's estimated value and were selling because of a certified PerPI situation, the government would make you whole. As you can imagine, that got abused pretty quickly.

I had no reason to sell; my neighbors and I could all see each other. There was one house at the end of the street where we could see the man but not the woman. They were renters and their lease was almost up, so they just stayed until it was done and then they left. Not sure where they went. Kind of difficult when you have a couple like that, where one can be seen and the other can't.

If you were just dating it wasn't so bad. You'd tell the person to meet you at a restaurant's Perception Post. If you could both see the HoPo, great. If not, end of date. It just made sense. But for the couples who were already together, married even, that had to be tough. You would have to find a neighborhood of families like you, accepting of you. And then businesses that were okay with these out-of-sync-couples. Not easy, I'm sure.

Anyway, it's been almost five years since the phenomena

started. We've all adapted pretty well to things. Violence is rare. Not unheard of, but not the norm like it was when we all started to sort. I read a few companies were developing eyeglasses that had some kind of coating enabling you to see everyone all the time. I didn't really look into it. Seems unnecessary. I mean, why bother? You have your places, your friends, do you need more? Sometimes I wonder what my old friends are up to, like Brett. I'm sure they're doing just fine. In the end, we've all got our things. Our circles. It's just easier this way.

* * *

This story first appeared in the After Dinner Conversation—July 2022 issue.

Discussion Questions

1. Assuming the phenomenon in this story were true, do you think people really would start to simply cluster together with "people they could see" as the story implies, in restaurants, relationships, and housing?
2. If you were in the situation in this story, do you think relationships you had with people you couldn't always see would start to fade away, or would you be able to maintain those relationships?
3. By the end of the story, there are glasses that allow someone to see everyone again, but the narrator doesn't want to use them. Why do you think that is? Why do you think the narrator is unwilling to accept and use such a simple piece of technology?
4. What analogies do you see in the story to culture today? Are there people we simply do not see? Who are they, and how might we overcome this issue?
5. If it is easier, and everyone is happier, spending time only with people they can see, then is there really a need to make the extra effort to see everyone? What, if anything, is gained by seeing everyone (*in the story, or in life*)?

* * *

The Angel In The Juniper

Sarah Johnson

* * *

Old Clyde Adamson was plotting with the Jacobin faction.

Holly, who had studied under him only the subjects he taught on the side—Neoplatonism in the early Church Fathers, and Classical Drama—had hired on a month ago as his secretary, and was now perfectly sure.

It was disturbing. One couldn't deny that the present republic had degraded to the mere form of representative government under the last president and his hand-picked parliament, but the Jacobins were dangerous—low-profile activists who had formally concluded that the governmental system no longer admitted renewal by legitimate means, and were prepared to incite even revolution to restore the principles of the four-hundred-year-old Constitution.

Holly didn't know yet how deeply Prof. Adamson was involved with the faction, or how high a member he might be.

She felt sure that, with his broad scholarly reputation and influence, he could hardly fail to be a decisive force in the group. But the thought that the boss she so liked and respected could be a treasonist, hardly alarmed her more than the inevitable, gastric knowledge that this brilliant man knew, or would very soon know, that she knew. And would address the fact, to protect himself and his party. Somehow.

That gastric knowledge turned to a squadron of armed butterflies when Prof. Adamson came in that morning and said quietly, "Miss Granger, I wonder if I can ask you to join me on a stroll into Warbell Wood this afternoon? I feel it's time I introduced you to someone there, someone closely involved in my work. Please don't be alarmed, Miss Granger. This can mean nothing personally harmful to yourself, unless you voluntarily choose to undergo certain risks in support of a noble cause. You are under no threat or duress of any kind—only the invitation to learn about something you may consider important."

While looking at his face—ever-same, good-humored yet earnest—she could not fear or distrust, and agreed; but when he had gone to his lecture hall, could do both with a vengeance. She told Mrs. Parsley, the bursar, where she was going that afternoon, and left a note instructing her to contact the police if Holly wasn't back by 10 p.m. (No use if the police had found something more profitable to do, like arresting a dissenter, but supposing they hadn't.)

Afternoon came, and so did Adamson.

"Take your coat, Miss Granger. And have you any heavier shoes? The going will be rough."

It was.

Holly was surprised to find how well Adamson seemed to

know his way, where there was no path, and how vigorously the old man could forge through the thick brush and bracken of this less-frequented part of Warbell Wood, a sylvan enclave that edged bustling Old Fruit Market Square, but, bottlenecked between two suburbs, eventually widened and stretched for miles into the hills. Holly thought herself athletic, but was frequently left several paces behind, gingerly poking at a spray of barbed hawthorn or caught by the stocking to a tough bramble.

It was easier here, amid a dense growth of dusty ferns; Holly kept easily by Adamson's side, and could even join in conversation. She had caught scraps of commentary through the branches, and knew he was trying to explain something about morality and the appeal to divine authority, but could only begin to pay attention now, in mid-lecture.

"I'm saying this because very soon, in about fifteen minutes, you'll meet a man who lives out here nearly all the time. Before I tell you what he does, I need to know your own conscientious view of the work of the Jacobin faction, with which you must be a little familiar. How do you..."

His voice trailed off through the foliage of a juniper while Holly was forced to stop and get a twig out of her shoe. She raised her head to call, "Please wait a moment, sir—"

And didn't call.

Holly had never seen an angel, but knew that was one sitting in the juniper tree. Flowing-haired and broad-jawed, hardly female, hardly male, picked out in a dazzling clarity that made the surrounding greenery seem blurred, it reclined on the branch with the easy balance of a seagull, a figure which seemed spatially paradoxic—compared to the branch, a miniature person, yet full of an aplomb that gave the impression of giantism.

"Holly."

She teetered a step nearer, still holding one shoe.

"Adamson is a traitor of the worst kind, Holly. He has turned against his own nation and the government that provided for his career, and is even now coordinating an armed rebellion, to break out in a few days. He is leading you to a meeting with an even more dangerous conspirator."

"Wh... what can I do?" lisped Holly.

"You must prevent the rebellion. Adamson's disappearance will paralyze the Jacobin communication network. You must kill him."

Holly staggered to the juniper's trunk and leaned, panting.

"Out here, before you get any closer to the radio shack where his accomplice works. Where no one will hear a sound. Since he joined the rebels, he always carries a sharp, double-bladed hunting knife in the breast pocket of his coat. Very soon it will fall accidentally on the ground. Watch for it, snatch it without his seeing, then carry it secretly until you see a chance to thrust it under his ribs. Hide his body in the bushes, then walk downhill until you find running water, which will lead you out of this wood. In two weeks, the search for him will expose some of his incriminating papers, which will prove beyond the slightest doubt that he was on the verge of inciting revolt. It is then you must announce your deed and reveal his body. You will save the peace, and all the lives that might be lost by warfare. You will receive the praise and thanks of your nation, and with good reason."

Holly pressed her closed eyes to the bark.

"Go, Holly. Great matters depend upon you. The time is short. God will speed and nerve you. Go, daughter!"

Hardly knowing what she was doing, Holly stumbled hastily through the branches, now following the voice she realized was Prof. Adamson's, and which was calling her name again and again. "I'm coming, sir!"

"You're tired," exclaimed Adamson anxiously when she appeared through the boughs. "I've hurried you too much. I'm sorry, Miss Granger. I was anxious that we would not be followed. I felt you could be trusted. I know your strong conscience, and your concern for good administration, in the college and in my office, and I feel sure you must hate the abuses of the present legislation. Do you read the leaflets by 'Socius,' the anonymous Jacobin writer?"

"I have, sir," murmured Holly. A disturbing memory. The little pink leaflets, occasionally appearing overnight on doorsteps or park benches and eagerly collected by public-minded citizens before the police could confiscate them, contained very little political commentary, but only excerpts from the secret minutes of the current Parliament, which revealed how deeply rotted with bribery and nepotism the lawmaking body had become. The State's frantic efforts, not to disprove, but suppress their content, was only too solid evidence of their accuracy.

Something glinted on the ground. As soon as Adamson turned to thrust forward among the beech saplings, Holly unthinkingly caught up the fallen knife and clutched it, under her coat against her pounding heart.

"What do you think of Socius?" asked Adamson, over his

shoulder. "What do you think of his contentions?"

Holly was too honest not to admit, "I have—I have found them very penetrating, sir. Very well-attested."

"And you agree," grunted Adamson, holding back a branch to allow her to pass, "that our system of suffrage and referendum has been narrowed almost to preclude the chance of reorganizing parliament or the presidency by legal means?"

This touched a sore place in Holly; her own voting privilege had been revoked for life, like so many others', when she let her Public Pedestrians' license lapse for just two months. "I... have to admit, it seems that way."

"Do you love our nation, Miss Granger?" Adamson had stopped, to look in her face. "Do you want to see our ancient constitutional rights restored?"

Oh, how wonderful that would be. No more night raids. No more drafts for ruinous foreign wars without popular consent. No more arbitrary, commerce-withering tolls and taxes... Old, forbidden subjects taught again in the college...

Oh, mercy. The angel, the knife.

Holly trembled all over before she could catch herself. Adamson took her arm. "My dear, are you well? I've exhausted you! Sit down, over here, on this root."

How he reminded her of her courtly old Great-Uncle Everard; how she wanted to confide her battle to the man she had just yesterday regarded as a pillar of dependability and wisdom. How could the angel call him a "traitor of the worst kind"? How much about him she must not know! If not for the angel, she would be utterly convinced by now that he was an ardent patriot, and a humanitarian driven only to the possibility of violent revolt by a far more violent tyranny. But, if God were on the side of the present regime...

"Sir, will you repeat what you were trying to tell me earlier, about moral decisions and divine authority? I think I'm ready to listen."

"Gladly, Miss Granger. I was telling you about Socrates' 'Euthyphro Dilemma.' Basically, it states that moral laws are often said to rest on God's authority, as in the Bible. Yet it's conceivable that God could order someone to do something obviously immoral, as in the case of Abraham ordered to sacrifice Isaac, or even schizophrenics who believe a voice in the head telling them to commit crimes. This dilemma is often used in academia to discredit a religious approach to moral problems.

"The trouble is, in the absence of divine authority, all moral law becomes a social, even at a more basic level *neurological*, construct. There's no appeal to abstract ethics, only to more common or historically affirmed patterns of behavior, sometimes the appeal to species survival, which always beggars the simple question—'Why?' ...So I remain a theistic moral agent. You see, I got around Euthyphro long ago."

"How, sir?" murmured Holly, half-unconsciously fingering a shape under her coat.

"Don't you see? The dilemma assumes that something or someone, making a claim to be the Creating Mind good enough to overcome all reasonable doubt in the hearer, demands an act which breaks the universally recognized moral laws every faith and culture attributes, or has attributed, to the Deity—the laws that forbid murder, and, and perjury, rape, infanticide, thievery and vandalism, acts a culture's code must always go to extraordinary lengths to justify under any circumstances!—Miss Granger, not all *violence* is immoral. In very unusual circumstances, passivity is immoral. I want you to think about that as we climb this hill. But the test of a so-called divine voice is rather simple—nothing demanding a plainly immoral act can be the God who made the rules! God cannot change His mind by definition. All that's changeable is temporary, while that from which the temporary, changing world sprang, must be eternal and changeless. Moreover, all evil itself is a secondary product, the perversion of an original good. The creator, however, cannot be secondary, but primary—therefore wholly good."

"Then what if," Holly was vexed and embarrassed to hear her own voice whine pleadingly, "what if something that made every other claim—something outside and independent of this physical world, something... like you say, *primary*, independent of space and matter, suggested—an act—that *seemed*, only *seemed*, a little off, and you couldn't be sure—what was really right—wouldn't you be safer to obey?"

"Wipe your face, you're perspiring," said Adamson, passing her a folded cotton handkerchief. "I hurried you too much. I knew it."

Holly buried her damp face in the cloth, then emerged as suddenly. "Sir, my question?"

"Is that even a question, Miss Granger? You aren't safer to obey an immaterial being. If we premise that God laid out moral laws, then you're safer to obey Him, or *them*, for they're the same thing."

Holly felt herself at last on sturdy grounds of objection. "Sir, I can't agree. You mentioned two necessary qualities of God—goodness, but also that independence of the changing, temporary world. If a being is independent like that, it must follow from your own statements that that being is good." Her dizziness now was a different kind, not terror but exaltation. She saw herself convincing the old academic that her heavenly messenger was legitimate. She saw herself avoiding murder by persuading him to fulfill the angel's command himself, by abandoning or betraying the Jacobins.

Adamson reached and pulled toward himself a delicate huckleberry sprig, faintly smiling.

"Are you nearly ready to go on, ma'am? It's not far now. Perhaps you've gathered by now why we're climbing this great hill to reach our destination."

Holly wasn't thinking about hills.

"Nearly ready, sir. A couple more minutes. Just tell me. If an obviously immaterial, independent, primary sort of being told you that—that, for instance, the Jacobin side was really in the wrong about our country's future, that leaving the current regime in place and—and trying to peaceably reform it were better, would you reconsider?"

"Do you think I'd reconsider if *you*, sitting on that root, told me positively that the Jacobins were mistaken and the regime were reformable? With no more supporting evidence? Just that? Seriously!"

Holly wanted for a second to hide her face again, then thrust her jaw out.

"But *I'm* not an angel!"

"What difference? Haven't you ever heard that the Devil is a perverted angel? Not all that's immaterial is God. Part of *you* is immaterial, but *you're* not God!"

She was not in a frame of mind to play exhaustion long, and jumped up. "Well, if it's not far, let's go."

"Wait, Miss Granger. I mustn't, I can't, reveal my contact out here or his work before I know where you stand regarding the work of the Jacobin society. If you're against the prospect of violent revolt, I'll walk you back to town before it gets any later."

"I'm in favor," she blurted, turning a straining face toward another juniper tree; "I'm in favor," she repeated more loudly, swinging her perspiring forehead toward him. "Let's go. I'm not tired at all." But when he rose, she made an urgent gesture and took his arm.

Adamson walked easily on the rising ground, lightly supporting her arm on his rigid elbow and sending earnest, good-humored glances over the hazel brush and young beeches, carrying his native land toward civil war with every stride, yet serene in the confidence of his own moral system, grounded upon a God he had never seen, in which he placed such confidence precisely *because* of the not seeing.

And at his side scrambled Holly, keeping very near his ribs and trying to make her hand bring the knife from her coat and shove it under them, ever more feverishly convinced of the morality of the act, grounded upon a God she had seen, in which she placed such confidence precisely *because* of the seeing.

* * *

This story first appeared in the After Dinner Conversation—April 2021 issue.

Discussion Questions

1. Professor Adamson references "Euthyphro's Dilemma," where Socrates asks Euthyphro, "Is the pious loved by the gods because it is pious, or is it pious because it is loved by the gods?" What does this phrase mean, and how does it relate to Holly's problem?
2. Like Abraham being asked to kill his own son, do we have an obligation to obey God, even when it goes against our moral code?
3. Professor Adamson argues the God's morality is, definitionally, unchanging and timeless. Do you agree that morality (*from God or otherwise*) is unchanging and timeless? How does Holly's answer to the question affect her choice?
4. The story cites the mass removal of voting rights, night raids, rising taxes, and the near impossibility of legally changing the government. What, if anything, would be the "last straw" that would cause you to take up arms to violently overthrow the government?
5. Professor Adamson argues "not all *violence* is immoral. In very unusual circumstances, passivity is immoral." Do you agree? Can you think of an example where passivity is immoral?

* * *

Seconds Last

P.G. Streeter

* * *

So I'm talking to Linus the other day. We're sitting on that bench—you know, the one across from the carousel. Of course, I say "the other day," like it's not always just *this* day, but you know what I mean. It feels like a while ago.

Anyway, I'm talking to Linus, the one people call The Professor. We go way back. Used to bring his car to my shop in Hartford in the late '90s. Good guy.

He asks me, "Do you know where we are?" As if this hasn't been discussed a thousand times before. As if it's not the one thing on everyone's mind. As if any of us knows for certain.

I play it as cool as I can. I say to him, "They say...well, you know what they say. But I'm no theologian."

"No," he says back to me, "I mean, what's it look like, from before?"

"They tell me it's Central Park," I say, "although I wouldn't know. Never been to New York, myself. Not back then, anyway." I take a moment to admire the cloudless blue sky and all those massive gray towers that cut through it so cleanly. The early autumn wind shuffles crisply through the trees surrounding us, blowing through green leaves that show hints of yellow. Over at the carousel, kids are laughing. The painted horses dance up and down as they spin, just like they always do. That music (in my head, it's just titled "Circus Music") plays on a loop. It's all one big loop, I guess—but it's pleasant enough.

The Professor speaks up. "Central Park as it was in 1978," he says. "Which is funny, because I didn't kick it until August of 2019." The guy outlived me by a decade, and he likes to get my goat by telling me about the preposterous things that have—according to him—happened since. It's all good fun, but I know somehow he's not here to egg me on this time. Instead, he's about to get philosophical. I don't like that nearly as much.

I want to make an excuse—maybe tell him I ought to go find my folks, see if they want to take a stroll through the zoo—but he pipes in too quickly. "It's from the first time I saw it," he says.

"Pardon?"

"When I was a young man, first trip to the city. Perfect day in early October—absolutely perfect. Makes sense that this would be my particular conceptual framework for it all. But it got me thinking: why would this be everybody else's schema? Everyone sees the same things here. Same trees, same skyline. Same hotdog vender, cheerfully slinging dogs even though he knows no one eats anymore. It's plucked right out of my past...so why would you all see my vision of it?"

"Listen, Linus, isn't that your family over there, sitting in the shade of that big old oak tree?" I can see them—his mom and pop, his wife and two boys. He told me once his parents beat him here by several years, but the wife and kids all got here the same time he did. Car accident, if I recall correctly. Tragic stuff, but it's nice to see them all together, I suppose.

"As a matter of fact," he tells me, grasping my arm now and staring straight into my eyes, "they're not my family. Not really. See, I've come to a revelation: I'm the only one here."

I can put up with Linus's philosophical discursions and mathematical ramblings, but I've got to admit it kind of stings to be told you're not real. I happen to be pretty convinced I exist, thank you very much. He sees it in my eyes, though, and he starts up again before I can say anything.

"I like you, Axel. You're good to talk to, even if you're just a projection from my memories, a spark of light from somewhere up here." He's pointing to his temple and twirling his finger a bit. Reminds me of the old gesture, the one meaning *loco*—which I'm beginning to think is pretty fitting.

"Linus," I say, but he cuts in again, in full-blown Professor mode now.

"See, I just can't bring myself to believe in the afterlife." He puts a finger to prevent my protest, then goes on: "I can believe, however, in the relativity of perception, especially in regard to time. You ever read about that burst of neural activity that occurs right before the brain dies?"

Matter of fact, I heard something like this on the radio, some years ago. "The fireworks," I say. "Fireworks in the brain, last thing you see."

"Yes. Like fireworks. A burst of light, because those neurons are firing like crazy." He pauses, then, "Do you know what an asymptote is, Axel?" I'm about to tell him I don't, but he just keeps on going: "See, I hypothesize that, in the moments preceding death, one's neural firing accelerates exponentially. It gets faster and faster, immeasurably so, and the mind processes things increasingly faster too."

"I'm not—" I start, but he cuts me off again. (Guess he doesn't care what I have to say—but why would he? I'm not real.)

He goes on: "In the precise moment before you die, what if your relative perception of time speeds up at an exponential rate? And because your processing speeds up, everything else slows down. Time moves forward, but from your perspective, you're never going to reach that line, the asymptote, the moment of death. And what can you perceive in such an infinitesimally small duration of time, except what's in your own mind, an endless delusion?"

"Linus—"

"It's nothing but an evolutionary quirk, perhaps, but it's an astounding one: we create our own afterlife. This is mine."

I pause and realize I'm sort of following. "But it can't last forever, can it? Eventually, time moves forward. You get to the point—the asymwhatsit."

He smiles like I'm not getting the joke, shakes his head. He looks around a moment, then gets a gleam in his eyes. "Ah. There it is," he says, and he points to another park bench, one that's got an advert across the seatback. *Fletcher Life Insurance*, the sign reads, with the agent's name, Z. Elea, underneath it in smaller letters. It's got a big red arrow streaking across a stark white background, hovering just short of a stylized bullseye on the far right of the placard.

The Professor goes at it again, and he's almost manic at this point, talking really fast, gesticulating a lot. "My mind must've added this little detail, a subliminal hint from my subconscious, you see?" I don't see, and I tell him so. He says, "To get to that bullseye, the arrow had to go half the distance first, then half that, and—"

"Oh, that old thing," I say. "Heard about that once. It was in a movie." And then it dawns on me: "You want to hit the target?" I pause, then add, "End the loop?"

He's dead silent, then nods solemnly. "It's not worth it if it's not real," he says, then slouches back onto the bench like a deflated balloon. We sit for a long time.

"But your family's over there," I say, eventually.

He seems not to hear me, just mutters, "I've got to do some calculations." Then he looks at me, smiles that off smile, says, "Maybe I can make my mind to slow down, you see. Quit accelerating, return to the relative flow of time." He gets out a little notepad and a ballpoint pen. Starts scratching.

I look at my old friend for a time—maybe a minute, maybe ages—and I wonder if he's onto something. I wonder if this'll be the last time I see him. I wonder if I'll still be here if he goes. Still... "Your family's over there, Linus. Under the oak tree."

He says nothing, and I get up from the bench without another word. I go off to find my folks, to see if they'll take a stroll with me through the zoo.

* * *

This story first appeared in the After Dinner Conversation—January 2022 issue.

Discussion Questions

1. They seem to be re-living the same pleasant moment*(s)* forever. Would you consider this heaven or hell? Why or why not?
2. If this is the last moment before Linus's death, stretched out forever, how is it that the story is written from the perspective of Axel?
3. Linus talks about the "relativity of perception." Do you think this "relativity of perception" happens in real life with various plants/animals? (*i.e. Hummingbirds think humans are moving at the speed of sloths.*)
4. Does something's being a delusion take away from its value? If you were Linus, would you simply stay in this happy place forever?
5. If you were to go to your happiest place, where (*and when*) would it be? What is it about a particular moment in time that makes it so pleasant?

* * *

Acceptance

Vinícius Gadini

* * *

October is the rainiest month of the year, the most unbearable month of the year. It is unbearable for those who need to leave the house to go to the bank, the market, the bakery. I had to go to the bank, to the market, the bakery. And I didn't have anyone to go for me, of course. But I didn't have a car and I depended on the weather to cooperate. The bastard was stubborn. Sunday, rain. Monday, rain. Tuesday, rain. Wednesday, rain. I was already upset. Thursday, rain. Friday, a miracle, the sun came out.

I left home with a new lease on life. I needed to buy bread. I walked through the streets with the speed of a hare. In the store windows, the fancy clothes of various brands dictated the way the rich beauties should dress. On car bumpers, stickers of politicians denounced that the municipal election and vote selling was approaching. In my earphones, Kanye West boasted this and that for all the world to hear. The world listened. The world was still the same, as it was before and as it would be after.

Nothing new under the sun.

I walked, walked, walked. It was a dirtier part of town. There was nobody there but me. The sidewalk was not finished, and what lay ahead was mud. A lot of mud. My shoes were filthy.

"HEEEY!"

I was startled when I saw it. I took off my earphones. I had almost tripped over a head emerging from the ground. Something new under the sun.

"But... what?"

"You almost fell on me."

"I'm sorry."

"It's okay, it's okay."

"What are you doing there?"

"Isn't it obvious?"

Maybe I was too dumb to notice the obviousness.

"I don't know. Is it?"

"Maybe it is."

He was a man around forty years old. He was up to his neck in a hole full of mud beside the sidewalk. He seemed to sink deeper and deeper, every second he sank another millimeter or so. I thought I had a duty to help him.

"I'm going to get you out of there."

"No!"

"Hold on. I'll call for help. I'll call the emergency."

"DON'T DO IT!"

The scream scared me.

"Won't you get out of there? You're sinking! You're going to die!"

He sneered.

"Seriously, man, you're going to die."

"Don't say it."

"You mean it's a suicide?"

"I didn't say that either."

"Then what? You're not going down? Is it a TV prank? Oh, I should have known! You know, I used to love watching these shows when I was younger. I'm finally going to be on TV. Where is it? Where's the camera? Oh, over there in that tree, right?"

"There isn't any camera."

"I want to see if there is."

There was no camera. There were branches, leaves, and some bugs, but no camera.

"So I don't understand. How did you get there?"

"Do you really want to know?"

I nodded.

"What is your name?"

"Vinicius."

"Well, Vinicius, since you are so keen to know, I fell here."

"You fell there?"

As he spoke, his neck sank deeper into the mud. He stood up so he could speak.

"I was walking. I was walking, I didn't see this here, I tripped and fell."

"How long have you been there?"

"Fifteen minutes, maybe."

"And nobody passed by here?"

"A woman and an old man did. They asked the same questions you did and tried to pull me by force. I didn't let them."

"And they left?"

"Yes, they left."

"But why don't you want help?"

"Why would I want help?"

"Come on, man, to save yourself."

"I don't want to."

"Don't be stupid. Come on, come on!"

I bent down to pull him up. I pulled as hard as I could. He began to struggle against me. He head-butted my hand.

"NO! I SAID NO!"

"I can't let you kill yourself like this!"

"I'm not killing myself!"

"How can you not, if you don't want to get out of this hole?"

"I do."

"Then let me help you."

"It doesn't matter what I want. It's what the universe wants."

"Don't be stupid! What are you talking about, man?"

It all seemed too absurd to me. He sank deeper and deeper.

"The universe wanted me to fall, the universe. And so I fell. There was no escape."

"And why doesn't the universe want you to save yourself?"

"I don't know. Ask him."

It was all absurd and ridiculous.

"And so," he continued, "what is left for me at this last moment is to accept the way the universe wanted me to die."

"Accept? Why? Why not fight?"

"I don't fight the universe. Acceptance is the best thing a human being can do. The world would be better, people would live in peace. The world would live in peace, there would be no more wars. One would just have to accept things, accept things the way they are, and not fight them."

"It sounds like self-indulgence to me."

"It doesn't matter if it is self-indulgence. Comfort is not bad if it works."

"I don't know what to say."

"Then don't say anything."

"You're going to die."

"So are you, yet you are gonna die, someday."

"Yes, but I'm not going to die sunk in the mud."

"What difference does it make to die sunk in the mud, to die from cancer in a hospital, to die in the war or in a plane crash? What difference does it make?"

"I don't know what difference it makes."

"Absolutely none! It makes no difference!"

He sank deeper. He had laid his head down to breathe a little more. His nose, eyes and mouth were all over the mud.

"Vinicius, do you like movies?"

"Do I like movies?"

"Do you like Woody Allen?"

"Very much."

"That's interesting."

"Do you like Woody Allen?"

"Not really."

He said this and sank to the bottom. His eyes, nose and mouth were swallowed by the murderous clay. His whole body disappeared into a grave of earth. For you are clay and to clay you shall return. I didn't even know his name.

I left the man of acceptance there. I looked around, there was no one. No one had seen me. I put on my earphones and kept walking. I needed to buy bread. In the store windows, chic clothes of various brands dictated the way the rich beauties should dress. In the cars, bumper stickers of politicians denounced that the municipal election and vote buying was approaching. In the earphones Kanye West praised God for this and that for the whole universe to hear. The universe listened. The universe remained the same, not giving a damn about that man who died respecting its will.

I went back home and tried to forget that face. I scratched my ass, ate bread and drank poor people's beer. I was poor. I accepted my condition imposed by the universe.

**

This story first appeared in the After Dinner Conversation—July 2022 issue.

Discussion Questions

1. Did the narrator make the right choice by refusing to help the sinking man, or did he have an obligation to help him even if he didn't want help?
2. The sinking man argues that the universe wanted him to fall into the hole and die (*i.e., fate*). Do you believe in fate? How do you know when something is "fate" vs. when you should act to change the situation? Isn't changing our situation the very nature of humanity and progress?
3. How do you know when to accept help and change your fate, and when to refuse it? What are the times *not* to accept help and change your fate?
4. Do you agree with the sinking man that, "Acceptance is the best thing a human being can do" and that acceptance would lead to world peace?
5. Are there times when it is better to simply accept a bad situation as the "will of the universe?" What would those types of situations look like?

* * *

Glad All Over

Lee Dawkins

* * *

The C30 cassette concluded with a terminal thud, plunging the darkened room back into silence. The lounge of Angus's small, terraced house, in a neglected and unfashionable part of South East London, was familiar to me, even in the gloom. I had sat on this scruffy old sofa countless times chatting with him. Our discussions ranged from the prosaic to the profound; from soccer—and our shared love of an equally neglected and unfashionable South East London football team—to philosophy and the meaning of existence. But nothing in any of those conversations prepared me for this moment. As I reached for my phone to call the emergency services, I recalled the day I'd first met Angus, almost exactly a year ago.

It was one of those really warm afternoons you sometimes get on the opening day of a new football season, when the conditions are more suited to cricket than soccer. The players of Crystal Palace Football Club, the Eagles, entered Selhurst Park stadium, walking out to the sound of their anthem,

"Glad All Over," blasting from the PA system. The Dave Clark Five were promising us truth, loyalty, and everlasting happiness. In response thousands of voices sang along, unanimously affirming that they were indeed feeling glad all over. A stout elderly man, his head topped with a froth of white curls, smiled as I wedged myself into the red plastic seat beside him. I was expecting a traditional South London greeting—a nod or maybe even an "All right, mate?"—so I was taken by surprise when, in an accent of a peculiar blend of Croydon and Glasgow, he said, "Epicurus taught that to enjoy a happy life, we should seek to avoid suffering." Holding out his hand he added, "I'm Angus, and I suspect we will be sharing more than a small amount of suffering, watching our beloved Eagles together this season."

It's always potluck who you end up sitting next to when you have a season ticket, but I immediately warmed to this fella. "It makes you wonder what we are doing here, doesn't it?" I replied.

Angus nodded thoughtfully. "I couldn't have put it better myself, son."

A few minutes into the game a quite unexpected thing happened; Crystal Palace took the lead. But it wasn't the goal that shocked me, it was my reaction to it. Instead of leaping to my feet in celebration as I would usually do, an unseen force pinned me to my seat. I was pleased we'd scored, but that was it, just pleased, nothing more. All around me people wildly punched the air. Complete strangers hugged each other. Few things in life invoke such raw emotion as soccer. Nothing else gets those neck veins bulging and nape hair bristling like this game. It's a truly unique feeling and one that has kept me coming back, season after season, for the last thirty-odd years.

But that *feeling* had now suddenly deserted me. The passion vanished, its place taken by a strange sense of disconnection, a numb detachment. I was surrounded by thousands of jubilant fans but had never felt more alone. Something was wrong. Very wrong. Anxiety rose as my heart began to race. My immediate impulse was to get out of the ground. I stood to leave.

"Excuse me, Angus," I said as I began my attempt to seek the sanctuary of the gangway. But instead of standing aside to let me through, he seemed to intentionally block my way.

"You're not off already are you, son? Quitting while we're ahead, eh?" Laughing loudly, he slapped me firmly on the shoulder, folding me back into my seat. He then began to talk and didn't stop talking until the halftime whistle. If you asked me what he'd said, I wouldn't have been able to tell you, but I do know I found his words comforting, and the panic gradually subsided. The halftime break was the perfect opportunity for me to make my getaway, but instead of heading for the exit, I found myself offering to get Angus a cup of tea. We continued our conversation in the second half, and the Eagles were polite enough not to interrupt our discussions by scoring another goal.

I spent the next couple of weeks trying to work out what had caused my meltdown.

Perhaps I'd just fallen out of love with football. My wife had been telling me for years that it was a silly game—twenty-two overpaid men running around kicking a bag of wind. Maybe I had finally and belatedly grown up? But if it was that simple, why had my reaction been so intense? I decided to give my season ticket away and have a break from the game. I could look at taking up a different hobby. Gardening is cool these days, or I could try working out, before my body becomes totally irredeemable. However, as the next home match drew nearer, these plans faded. Bizarrely I found myself actually looking forward to going to the game. But I realized it wasn't the football attracting me, it was the thought of meeting up again with Angus.

Men are encouraged to be more open about our mental health these days, but baring your soul to a total stranger who just happens to sit next to you at a sporting event is still a tall order. Nevertheless, I felt surprisingly at ease when I confided in Angus at the following game. It didn't take him long to establish that this wasn't just a football thing, it reflected how I was feeling about life in general: work, family, everything. After hearing me out, he delivered his verdict; I was undergoing an existential crisis. I wasn't sure what it was, but it sounded a lot sexier than a boring old midlife crisis. Sensing my uncertainty, Angus ran through a checklist: Lack of purpose? Yes; Sense of isolation? Got it; Absence of meaning? 100 percent; Awareness of own mortality? You bet. I ticked every box. I was facing the classic paradox of someone who thinks life is important, while simultaneously believing it has no purpose. I must have looked worried, because Angus was quick to reassure me that my crisis was a perfectly natural response. We are hardwired to search for meaning, he explained, but everyday life gets in the way. Grappling with the technicalities of a 3-5-2 team formation over a midfield diamond is hard enough, without having to consider free will, the nature of the self, or proving the existence of an external world. But fundamental questions have a habit of bubbling to the surface in some of us, and when they do, they are impossible to ignore.

So, if that was the diagnosis, what was the cure? It was at

an evening game against Manchester City when Angus told me about Antiphon the sophist and his "Shop of Consolation" in ancient Corinth. Above the door was the inscription, *"I can heal illness with words."* Angus revealed that he had suffered a crisis of his own many years ago and had found solace in words. His crisis had been precipitated by a heart-breaking tragedy—the death of his only child from viral meningitis at the age of just nine. Philosophy had saved Angus. He stumbled by chance on a story about the pre-Socratic Greek Anaxagoras. Legend has it that upon being told that his sons were dead, Anaxagoras calmly replied that he knew his children were born to die. These simple words gave Angus strength. They also inspired him to read the great philosophers and embark on a lifetime quest for understanding.

The wisdom he accumulated had recently been helping him through another devastating event, his wife's dementia. Ruth had introduced Angus to Crystal Palace shortly after he'd swapped Glasgow for London in the '60s. Until she became unwell, she accompanied him to every game. He refused to consign her to a care home, insisting on looking after her himself in their own house. He received very little assistance, but a kindly neighbor popped in to cover for him when needed. Fortunately for me, the neighbor thought it would do Angus good to continue going to football.

There is an old Buddhist proverb that says, *"When the student is ready, the master appears."* Angus offered to share his learning with me, and I jumped at the chance. I warned him that the closest I'd got to reading any philosophy was the *"Live. Laugh. Love."* sign in our kitchen. Angus assured me that the only entry qualification to his impromptu course was an open mind.

So, match days became a symposium as Selhurst Park was transformed into my personal Lyceum. Each football game featured a masterclass on a different philosopher or school of thought. It was enthralling. Angus had a way of making difficult ideas seem simple. For the first time in my life, I enjoyed learning. The fixtures couldn't come quickly enough. Soon we were meeting for extra-curricular sessions over a pint of London Gold at Angus's local pub, the Crown and Sceptre, or a cuppa at his house. He was clear with me from the start that this wouldn't provide an off-the-peg blueprint for living the perfect life. He said if I wanted that, I should seek the ministrations of a priest. Nor did this learning come with a money-back guarantee that I'd find any answers. In fact, the most valuable lesson Angus taught me was that the questions themselves are as important as the answers. It's not just the destination, but the road you take. Even if life is ultimately unknowable, the quest for understanding, no matter how futile, is still an edifying one.

If you had asked me twelve months ago about Albert Camus, you would have been met with the blankest of stares. Thanks to Angus, I now know that Camus not only said some pretty profound things but was also a very decent goalkeeper—though whether he ever managed to perform both these feats at the same time, only his back four would know. Angus wanted to show me that philosophy was for everyone, not just intellectuals. It was as relevant for football fans as it was for academics. Camus combined playing the beautiful game with applying his beautiful mind to the purpose of life. Without meaning, Camus thought life was absurd. It's an absurdity that can ambush us anywhere: a street corner, a sun-blasted beach, a football match. And when it strikes, we must confront it, embrace it, live with it. Finding happiness then becomes a duty, a moral obligation. Angus said we should find happiness wherever we can: in art, in nature, in friendship, in love, and, yes, in sport.

After all, it was Camus himself who said, "What I know most surely about morality and obligations I owe to football."

Angus rattled off a list of things that gave him pleasure. It was an eclectic inventory, a mixtape of personal joys: country walks with Ruth, a traditional English fry-up, *The Hay Wain* by John Constable, a vinyl copy of *Kind of Blue*, quantum entanglement, the smell that follows a shower of rain, his battered edition of the *Nicomachean Ethics*, any film with Fred MacMurray, a decent pint of London Gold and, of course, cheering on the Palace as they walk out to "Glad All Over." These pleasures don't just add meaning—they are the meaning.

By the final game of the season my crash course in 2,500 years of western philosophy had taken me from the pre-Socratics of the ancient world to Plato, then on to the Cynics, the Stoics, the Skeptics, and the Epicureans. We had traveled through the medieval and Renaissance thinkers to Descartes and the modern age. There we met Schopenhauer, Nietzsche, Kierkegaard, and Sartre. Thanks to Angus, I am now familiar with epistemology, metaphysics, and empiricism. I know my Aristotle from my Hegel, my Berkeley from my Kant. Along the way, I was introduced to thought experiments involving evil demons, and cats that were simultaneously dead and alive. It was truly revelatory. Angus's love of knowledge and understanding was infectious; and while he'd been right to warn me it was no short-term fix, I was definitely feeling an awful lot better in myself. And Crystal Palace hadn't been playing too badly either.

I saw Angus regularly during the off-season. His mood was typically buoyant despite a worrying downturn in Ruth's condition. Whenever we met, he was as passionate as ever, always eager to introduce me to new ideas he thought I would enjoy.

Punctuality was one of Angus's many qualities, so when he didn't show up at the pub on time this evening, I suspected something was wrong. I walked the short distance to his house. The front door was open, and there was no sign of anyone inside. The lounge curtains were drawn, but once my eyes had adjusted to the dark, I saw an old-fashioned cassette recorder on the coffee table. Next to it was a note in Angus's distinctive script. It simply said, *"Play me."* I pressed the start button with trepidation. Nostalgic hisses and crackles filled the room as the magnetic tape started to revolve. Then Angus's voice was addressing me. He told me not to be alarmed—which immediately alarmed me—and warned me not to go upstairs. I sensed this was not going to end well. My worst fears were quickly confirmed when Angus broke the shocking news. He instructed me to inform the police that Ruth's body could be found in their bedroom. His own body, he added casually, would be lying next to hers. Surely this wasn't true. I wanted it to be an elaborate philosophical thought experiment that Angus had devised to demonstrate one of his ideas. If I went back to the Crown and Sceptre, I would be sure to find him there in his favorite chair sipping a pint of London Gold. The cassette continued to revolve, and Angus continued his monologue. I realized this was no experiment.

"What have you done Angus?" I shouted into the darkness with a mixture of anger and remorse. What right did he have to take Ruth's life? And how did it help by taking his own when he had so much more to give? He answered me by first explaining in cool and dispassionate terms exactly what he was about to do. He spoke without emotion, as if he was reading out the assembly instructions of a piece of flat-pack furniture. His tone changed when he turned to *why* he was doing it. Ruth had always been afraid of death. She was especially scared of dying alone. While the thought of death didn't bother Angus, he understood his wife's fear. Nothing he said ever gave her reassurance, so, many years ago, he promised that if she was ever facing death, then they would die together. Ruth took great comfort from his words, and although most of her memories had been erased in the fog of her disease, she had never forgotten that promise. Angus realized that her time was fast approaching, and if he was to honor his word, he would need to act now. When he told her what he was going to do, she smiled. It was a smile he knew so well, but which he had not seen in a very long time. And he knew when he saw it that he was doing the right thing. His voice was still calm, almost serene, but now with just an edge of emotion. It was not how I imagined a man who was about to take the life of his wife of nearly sixty years as well as his own would sound. There was no trace of doubt, no hint of any moral reservation. He was as certain he was doing what was right as any man could be.

Angus ended the recording with these words:

"Please do not mourn for me, son. I was born to die. I have lived my life to the full and found plenty of happiness along the way. I am now happy that it should end here. And happy too that my ending will bring comfort to the person I love the most as she passes. My epitaph will be the Epicurean epitaph: *Non fui;*

fui; non sum; non curo—I was not; I was; I am not; I do not care."

The analog hiss of late twentieth-century technology resumed. I was about to press *eject* when suddenly I heard the familiar voices of The Dave Clark Five. They were promising a love that lasts for eternity. And they were feeling glad all over.

* * *

I have just finished scattering Angus's and Ruth's ashes on hallowed ground, at the hallowed ground. Just behind the Holmesdale Road stand at Selhurst Park is a little patch of grass reserved for the remains of Eagles fans who have gone to take their seat in the great stadium in the sky. Soccer is the closest thing Angus had to a religion, so I thought it was a fitting resting place. It's the first day of another new season and the sun is shining on cue. As I head to my usual seat, I still half expect to see those distinctive white curls greeting me. It feels strange to find an unfamiliar face sitting in his place. It makes Angus's passing feel more real. His substitute, a man in his twenties, sees me approaching and gives me a nod. "All right, mate?" he says as I sit down next to him.

I am tempted to shake his hand and offer a quote from Epicurus. I settle instead for a reciprocal, "All right?"

As the players take to the field Dave Clark and his four friends launch into "Glad All Over." I look at all the people standing around me. They are clapping and singing along; experiencing the simple pleasure of being part of something that transcends the individual self. For a few brief moments all their troubles, all their worries, all their frustrations are forgotten. They are happy. And in this instant, I see things with an exquisite clarity. I know that I too have every reason to be happy; to be feeling glad all over.

Five minutes into the game something quite unexpected happens—Crystal Palace take the lead. It isn't the goal itself that shocks me, but my reaction to it. A surge of excitement runs through my body, spontaneously propelling me out of my seat and onto my feet. I turn to the lad next to me and give him the biggest hug I've ever given any stranger at a football match. The noise is deafening, so he doesn't hear me shouting to Angus through my tears. "You were not; you were; you are not; I care."

* * *

This story first appeared in the After Dinner Conversation—March 2023 issue.

Discussion Questions

1. Angus introduces himself by saying, "Epicurus taught that to enjoy a happy life we should seek to avoid suffering." What does this mean, and do you agree?
2. Later, Angus explains that "Without meaning, Camus thought life was absurd." What does this mean, and do you agree?
3. Angus defines an existential crisis as a (1) lack of purpose (2) sense of isolation (3) absence of meaning and (4) awareness of your own mortality. What is the difference (*if any*) between an existential crisis and a midlife crisis?
4. What would be your advice to a friend or family member suffering from an existential crisis?
5. Do you think Angus did the right thing by killing his wife and taking his own life? Once his wife was dead, why did Angus also decide to kill himself? Do you think any *(or all)* of this was the right choice?

* * *

I Do So, Like Durian

Jann Everard

* * *

The 504-streetcar grated against the curve of the tracks as it entered the station. It pulled to a stop directly in front of Holly. The doors opened with such a clunk that she stepped back, treading on the toes of the person behind her. She was blocking the door. A crowd of restless Chinese grandmothers nudged her forward with sharp elbows.

"Does this car go south on Broadview?" she asked the driver. He adjusted his seat and the booklet of transfers clipped to the dash. He didn't bother to look at her. "504 turns at Queen, 505 at Dundas," he said.

"But does it go south?" she persisted, and he flicked a thumb to the back of the car, signaling for her to board.

She had never been to Broadview Station before. She rarely used public transit. Her high school was within walking distance of her house. And her mother was happy to drive her wherever she and her friends wanted to go. "I don't like you girls alone on public transit," she'd say, the slight wrinkle of her nose suggesting that the matter wasn't so much about safety. "Besides, driving together gives us a little time to chat." She would perch on the edge of Holly's bed until the silence from Holly's friends went on a little too long.

Somewhere south of the station was the restaurant where Jon worked. Holly had tried to tease the name out of him but he'd evaded her. "It's downtown, not anywhere near where you live," he'd said. "Besides, you told me you only liked sushi and Italian from the Village." She'd pressed, scooting closer to him on the bench in the library where she kept him company while he studied at lunch. "I just want to know where you are on Friday nights," she said, her hand brushing his arm. His temptation was palpable, but while Holly silently pleaded for him to make a move, his lips stayed grimly set and his attention returned to his textbook. "It's on Broadview, near Gerrard," he conceded.

East Chinatown. Her mother would never agree to drive her there. She hated Chinese food and had always rejected the idea of trying dim sum when Holly had suggested it. "God knows what goes in those odd-looking dishes," she said. "Chinatowns everywhere smell of dried shrimp and rotting vegetables and the people are loud and pushy and—" She'd caught herself then, perhaps realizing how she sounded or that negativity made her inelegant. "I don't like that neighborhood, Holly, dear."

But Holly liked Jon. Liked the leanness of him, the smooth toffee of his skin and the taut arrow of his ambition. It felt as if he had bypassed the teenaged years and already knew something more about life. With Jon, she could almost see herself as an adult. Confident. Knowing. With him, a relationship could move past Friday nights chilling with friends, vodka shots and inexperienced groping.

Holly texted Sasha to tell her she'd left Broadview Station and eyed the people around her to see if there was anyone she knew—anyone that might report Holly's whereabouts to her mother, who would surely ground her for lying or impose a curfew. Sasha had agreed to be her cover if Holly's mom got unexpectedly curious, but only on the condition that Holly texted every detail of her evening. She was thumbing a long message about the rude driver when she heard the streetcar's announcement system call out Queen Street. The driver had said the car turned at Queen. She rushed to the front.

"Have we passed Gerrard?" On Google maps, Broadview Avenue had appeared long. She'd been so focused on her text to Sasha that she hadn't noticed how fast the car was moving.

"Gerrard was a couple streets back," said the driver, his tone flat, his eyes dead ahead. He sounded the bell and swore lightly at some rowdy pedestrians who swarmed off the sidewalk at the Queen Street corner, blocking what was already a tight turn. As he waited for people to move, he said to Holly, "You can walk back. It'll only take you about ten minutes." He opened the door and let her out, taking advantage of the opportunity to call, "Get out of the way, you crazy bunch of drunks!"

Holly sidestepped a group loitering in the glow of a streetlamp, avoiding eye contact. When she looked up, she was in front of three girls with large, exposed breasts—posters on a brick wall. A couple of guys in toques smoked nearby. Their eyes raked over her, brash, hungry, but dismissive. Above their heads, *Jilly's Exotic Dancing* glowed in neon. Holly turned on her heel to cross the street, clutching harder to her Coach bag, running to catch the last few seconds of the warning countdown of the pedestrian light.

The pattern of black and white splotches painted on the outside of the restaurant on the opposite corner was meant to suggest the hide of a Holstein and, by extension, beef burgers, she guessed. As Holly passed the steamed-up windows, she glimpsed five or six patrons inside laughing while making crude sexual gestures and planned to text Sasha that all the people on this corner were lowlifes. For now, though, it was better to keep her phone in her pocket.

She took a glimpse at her watch. 8:30. She still had time to find Jon's restaurant. He wasn't off work until 9:00, although he'd told her that even after he'd finished serving customers, there was still plenty of work to do and he wouldn't be able to meet her. "If you're off work you should be able to go," she'd pointed out, and he'd looked at her—was the look impatient? She couldn't always tell what Jon was thinking—and said, "I'm expected to stay."

Holly twitched the zipper of her jacket a little higher. It was a crisp evening and she was wearing only a bra top with spaghetti straps underneath. Her friends—Sasha too—would be going to an all-ages dance club later, near where she lived in midtown. She'd put on the top hoping that Jon might agree to meet her friends there, to take a break, for her sake. She wanted him to dance with her. To hook up with her, finally. Or they could go some place else. It didn't really matter as long as they spent part of the evening together. Up until now, they had mainly walked in the neighborhood parks during spares, talking about college, life after high school. The top's tight fabric, rubbing against her nipples, made her feel self-conscious and more forward than she'd intended. What if people walking toward her could tell how little she had on under her zipped-up jacket? What if Jon thought her outfit was over the top for a first date, slutty even? She kept her hand on the zipper of her expensive jacket, her arm hiding its logo.

Not far from the cow restaurant she noticed a northbound streetcar stop. She had no tickets or tokens, only three twenty-dollar bills her mom had given her for the weekend. Public transit drivers didn't make change; she'd have to walk. Her feet didn't hurt too badly yet, despite her heeled boots. Ten minutes, the driver had said. Acrid smoke from a cigarette made her speed up past a woman sitting on a cement half-wall. The woman had no coat and pulled on the cigarette so hard her cheeks caved hollowly.

The aroma of fresh bread floured the air and voices drew her attention to a bakery with its front door open. An Asian man in a dirty apron stood outside, facing the street, backlit by the bakery lights. He was young and looked a little like Jon. Like Jon, but not as attractive.

"Gerrard's not far, is it?" she asked.

"Yeas, yeas," he replied, as if chewing on the word. "First you go right." He gestured with his hand northward and then with a small head bobble to the left said, "And then you go right."

These directions confused her, but she decided not to press. Two very tall men in the bakery were looking her way, eyes narrowed. She was interrupting their work.

After the bakery, Holly passed a row of six Victorian row houses with stained glass windows and wrought-iron fences, a low apartment block, a school. This felt better. The houses were narrow, a quarter of the size of the homes in her neighborhood, but they had nice gardens. But then the businesses got shabby again. A few were permanently closed. The smell of garbage, heaped in piles, permeated the air, as did cooking oil. Looking down a few stairs directly to her right, there was a bent woman in a hairnet carrying an industrial-sized tray. Dumplings made in a basement. Her mother's words came back to her.

Ahead was a corner variety store, a subway sandwich joint, a single man in a dark hoodie shrouded by the scented smoke of marijuana standing in front of the kind of coffee place Holly would never enter, the lowest on the coffee franchise food chain. The strip was otherwise deserted; Holly's footsteps echoed alone.

This couldn't be where Jon worked, not near an area like this. Where were the shops and clothing stores? Her cellphone vibrated in her pocket but she didn't remove it. She hadn't texted her friend in ten minutes or more. Sasha would be wondering why. Knowing Sasha was waiting for her to make contact gave her courage. With one press of a button, she could have her on speakerphone. She could tell her that this place was seedy. Or not. She could handle this alone. Sasha didn't have to know everything.

In the block above Dundas were a Mission-run secondhand shop and unkempt businesses that had signs in Chinese with English translations beneath. The 505 streetcar sped south and squealed as it took the corner onto Dundas heading west. It blew dried leaves across the pavement and stirred up a grit-storm in its wake. An ugly institutional block of what could only be subsidized housing butted up to the sidewalk, small high windows hung with red and gold medallions. She looked at them knowing she had no idea if they were religious or merely decorative. Jon would know. She'd ask him.

She could finally see the streetlights of the Broadview-Gerrard intersection ahead. The block was bright with signs, red on yellow, yellow on red, all in Chinese characters. It was crowded; the sidewalk narrowed by more garbage bins and collapsed cardboard boxes on the left, and people and produce spilling out of the stores on the right. A friend had said there were only a few restaurants on Broadview, that most faced Gerrard. Holly's plan had been to unobtrusively look in each one until she found Jon. But there was no way she could be unobtrusive here.

This was not what she'd expected. She didn't know what she'd expected. She'd expected something different, more familiar than this. It hadn't occurred to her that Jon's life was still so connected to his cultural roots. He went to her school, after all, in a neighborhood far from this. Lots of kids did travel from around the city to her school. Smart kids. Gifted kids, like Jon. It had always been his smartness, his studiousness, that had defined him, not his Asian-ness.

She stopped before she had waded too far up the block and looked up at the signs again. Sing BBQ Restaurant. Ka Ka Lucky Seafood BBQ Restaurant. She looked at that one again. Had they no idea? Poor Jon, if he worked in the Ka Ka Lucky Seafood BBQ Restaurant.

She was pushed closer to a tier of boxed fruits and vegetables. Next to her was a pile of large, football shapes—she didn't know if they were fruits or vegetables. They looked armored, covered in dull, drab-colored spikes. She turned to a fellow who was stacking oranges and gestured.

"What is this?" she asked.

He answered, but she couldn't mimic his response. "Pardon?" she prompted.

A younger woman beside her answered. "Is durian. Smell." She held one of the fruits closer to Holly's nose and, even as it approached, she could tell she was going to gag from the odor. The woman looked away, smirking a little.

Holly straightened her shoulders and glared at the woman. If she didn't know a durian, it wasn't because she was ignorant or disinterested. She wanted to know durian and that stack of tubers there and that heap of green vegetables next to her here. Defiant, she grabbed a plastic bag from the roll above the oranges and shoved into it the largest durian from the pile, knotting the plastic closed. She strode into the store and held out a twenty to the young girl at the till, who took the bill and returned change without expression.

The next business was a small restaurant. It glowed with the bluish light of old-fashioned fluorescent tube lighting. The walls were the color of a school bathroom, the tables streaked to show the direction of each wipe of a dirty washcloth. Four or five patrons sat scattered around the room watched over by a woman who stood with her weight shifted onto her right hip as if it were too painful, or required too much energy, to stand straight. High in the window hung dead birds, their cooked skins glistening and crisp. At the back, in a filthy apron stood Jon, his expression closed. The plastic tub he held brimmed over with dishes smeared with jelled sauce and flecks of rice and noodle. A door beside him was propped open to reveal the carcass of a pig, hanging in its entirety, from a metal hook in the ceiling.

For a second, panic brewed in Holly's stomach. She

desperately wanted to be somewhere else. Someplace dim. Someplace anonymous. Just to think about what all this meant. To practice a reaction. But what reaction? Jon wasn't wearing the white-shirt-black-pants uniform of the servers at the kind of restaurants she was used to but cheap, shiny polyester. The smells weren't anything she was used to either. The area was poor and chaotic, the restaurant plain.

But it was also exotic. Her parents had never brought her to a place like this. She'd arrived here by herself. Her choice. And everything was so totally outside her experience that it felt like a small act of rebellion. Liking Jon had already made her see differently in some ways. Before she'd met him, her future had felt blurry with the soft edges of entitlement. His was sharply defined by a hunger to get on with it, to make life happen. Success wasn't inevitable in Jon's mind—it had to be manufactured. That's what made him so attractive to Holly—the intensity with which he worked for what he wanted. She wanted him to show that same intensity to be with her. She'd show him she could step up to a challenge too. The defiance that had compelled her to buy the durian propelled her through the restaurant's front door. Jon looked up, his forehead furrowed.

"What are you doing here?" he asked.

His embarrassment stiffened her resolve. "I'd like to eat." She glanced at the woman. "I'd like to try this. I hope it doesn't need much cooking." She held out the plastic bag containing the durian. This set off a long flurry of conversation between the woman and Jon. She waited. "Is your boss okay with that?"

"She's not my boss. She's my mother. You won't like the flavor of this." Jon peeled off his apron and approached, reaching for the bag. It was heavy; her shoulder was beginning to ache from holding it out. She turned toward Jon's mother. "I'm Holly. I'm pleased to meet you."

"She doesn't speak English." He held the bag gingerly. "This—" he considered, his glance bouncing around the room, "is an acquired taste."

"I'd like to try it anyway." Incredibly, her sense of confidence kept growing. "How do I say hello to your mother in her language?"

John shook his head. He pulled out a chair. "Sit here. I'll prepare it for you." Holly ignored him, smiled hard at his mother.

"But I'd like to see how to prepare it myself. Can't I go to the kitchen with you?" She made gestures, pointing at the back, mimicking the slice of a knife, holding Jon's mother's eyes, trying to win her over.

The woman, who had straightened, grew animated. She thrust her chin at the back of the restaurant and chattered to Jon. He argued, but relented once she moved toward them, sweeping them toward the kitchen door with flicks of her hands.

Holly grabbed the discarded apron from the back of the chair where Jon had dropped it and pulled it over her head. He was ahead of her, leading the way into the kitchen. As she was about to pass the pig carcass, she stopped, put her hands on its sides and did a little dance step that made the carcass sway on its hook. She didn't bother to look back into the restaurant. If anyone asked about her evening she could say she had gone dancing. But what anyone thought if they saw her here didn't really matter anymore.

* * *

This story first appeared in the After Dinner Conversation—June 2021 issue.

Discussion Questions

1. Holly's mother seems to have an exceptional dislike for Chinese culture and Chinatown. Why do you think that is? Why doesn't Holly share that dislike?
2. Holly seems to find Chinatown interesting and is willing to embrace it. Would her mother's reaction be different? If so, why?
3. Does it matter that Holly's reason to expand her cultural horizon is simply to talk to a boy she is interested in? Are there better or worse reasons to try new things?
4. What keeps Holly's mother from embracing new experiences? Is there anything you can do to keep that from happening to you?
5. When Holly's mother finds out Holly went to Chinatown, they will likely fight over it. What will be the result of that fight? What is likely the result of Holly and Jon's dating? Is it possible for Holly's mother to handle the situation differently/better?

* * *

Author Information

Home For The Holidays

Alexis Dubon spent most of her adult life waiting tables until quarantine, when, removed from all the real people out in the world, she decided to make up some new ones to keep her company. You can find her in *Home*, *Cosmos*, and *Beneath*, from the Hundred Word Horror anthology series by Ghost Orchid Press, on Crystal Lake Publishing's Patreon. X (Twitter) *@shakedubonbon*.

Abrama's End Game

David F. Shultz writes speculative fiction and poetry from Toronto, Canada, where he runs the 580-member *Toronto Science Fiction and Fantasy Writers* group, and is lead editor at *TDotSpec*. His more-than-fifty published works are featured or forthcoming through publishers such as *Abyss & Apex*, *Third Flatiron*, and *Diabolical Plots*. *www.davidfshultz.com*

Rose-Tinted Glasses

Ann has always been one of those adults who is told they should write children's stories for a living. Whilst this is usually a polite way of telling someone to daydream less, Ann took it to heart and let her imagination run rampant. Ann takes inspiration from myths, her own experience, and colorful dreams. X (Twitter) *@EntracteM*

The Big, Immovable, I

Harrison V. Perry is a writer, programmer, wannabe-philosopher, and part-time skateboarder, who lives with his partner, Lianne, and their two kitties Ed and Rex, in the sunny South East of England. *www.warpedandtorn.io*; X (Twitter) *@harrison_perry*

Sort of Polarity

Michael Klein is originally from New York but has called Northern Virginia home since 1999. He enjoys contemplating questions of morality, ethics, human nature, and existential crises with his dog, cat, and wife, and occasionally manages to pull their twenty-something children into the discussions from their homes in New York and Boston. He has run a writers group in the area since 2006 and feeds off the creative, collaborative, and combative camaraderie.

The Angel In The Juniper

Sarah Johnson is a writer, homemaker, and college sophomore from Washington State. Love of history, philosophy, and the forest all trickle into her wordcraft, which also appears in *Cassandra Voices*, *Solum*, and *The Chinook Observer*. She dreams of being a Professor of Church History, and of writing the Great Austrian-But-Written-by-an-American Novel.

Seconds Last

P.G. Streeter lives with his wife and two sons in Maryland, where he teaches high school English. His prior publications include work in Electric Spec, Daily Science Fiction, and StarShipSofa.

Acceptance

Vinícius de O. Gadini is a 19-year-old literature student who lives in Brazil and loves to experiment the possibilities of human life through poetry and short stories. He has been published in minor circles of Brazilian literature and would like to expand his view worldwide. His greatest influences are Hemingway, Fernando Pessoa and Jorge Luis Borges.

Glad All Over

Lee Dawkins is a lawyer and writer, with a degree in politics. He was born in London and now lives in the South West of England with his wife, daughter and a crazy Labradoodle. Lee writes across a range of genres, including literary, speculative and philosophical fiction. He is the proud owner of George Orwell's stapler.

I Do So, Like Durian

Jann Everard's fiction has been published in Canada, the United States, and New Zealand in journals including The New Quarterly, the Los Angeles Review, Whitefish Review, and Geometry. She was the winner of The Malahat Review's 2018 Open Season award for fiction. Jann divides her time between Toronto and Vancouver Island. *www.janneverard.com*

Additional Information

Reviews

If you enjoyed reading these stories, please consider doing an online review. It's only a few seconds of your time, but it is very important in continuing the series. Good reviews mean higher rankings. Higher rankings mean more sales and a greater ability to release stories.

Print Books

https://www.afterdinnerconversation.com

Purchase our growing collection of print anthologies, "Best of," and themed print book collections. Available from our website, online bookstores, and by order from your local bookstore.

Podcast Discussions/Audiobooks

https://www.afterdinnerconversation.com/podcastlinks

Listen to our podcast discussions and audiobooks of After Dinner Conversation short stories on Apple, Spotify, or wherever podcasts are played. Or, if you prefer, watch the podcasts on our YouTube channel or download the .mp3 file directly from our website.

Patreon

https://www.patreon.com/afterdinnerconversation

Get early access to short stories and ad-free podcasts. New supporters also get a free digital copy of the anthology *After Dinner Conversation–Season One*. Support us on Patreon!

Book Clubs/Classrooms

https://www.afterdinnerconversation.com/book-club-downloads

After Dinner Conversation supports book clubs! Receive free short stories for your book club to read and discuss!

Social

Connect with us on Facebook, YouTube, Instagram, TikTok, Substack, and Twitter.

Milton Keynes UK
Ingram Content Group UK Ltd.
UKHW011843120424
441050UK00004B/296